the villa

Sarah Sands is the editor of the *Sunday Telegraph*. She is the author of two previous novels, *Playing the Game* and *Hothouse*, and lives in London with her husband and three children.

Also by Sarah Sands

PLAYING THE GAME

HOTHOUSE

the villa

sarah sands

PAN BOOKS

First published 2006 by Pan Books
an imprint of Pan Macmillan Ltd
Pan Macmillan, 20 New Wharf Road, London N1 9RR
Basingstoke and Oxford
Associated companies throughout the world
www.panmacmillan.com

ISBN-13: 978-0-330-43326-6
ISBN-10: 0-330-43326-1

1 3 5 7 9 8 6 4 2

A CIP catalogue record for this book is available
from the British Library.

Typeset by SetSystems Ltd, Saffron Walden, Essex
Printed and bound in Great Britain by
Mackays of Chatham plc, Chatham, Kent

For Henry, Rafe and Tilly

Thanks to Hazel Gilbertson for her sound advice and good heart, and to Trisha Jackson for her work.

One

Before Jenny began her affair with Richard Wentworth she would unhesitatingly have described herself as one of the girls. The PAs at Meyer Gordon Stryker Shroeder (MGSS) were a community. They went drinking together – a quick one mid week and a pub crawl all the way to Accident and Emergency on a Friday – they saw films, did the sales, covered the phones for each other, had a laugh, exchanged secrets. Of course they were discreet about company matters, refusing to confirm or deny to outsiders. They had a sense of corporate pride sometimes absent in their bosses. They were puzzled by the subversive jokes they heard in the lifts about the members of the board whose dignified yet vigorous headshots appeared on the front of the laminated company brochure.

As with all communities there was a hierarchy among the PAs based on empirical evidence of hours, productivity and experience rather than capricious promotion. You worked your way up slowly, but were fired very suddenly since your fortunes were your own but your misfortunes were your boss's.

There was a wide margin of error in the valuation of top managers' worth. The worth of PAs was easier to judge – around 10 per cent of the boss's salary. Apart from the differences in salary and status, the PAs and their bosses were evenly matched on hours and work load. The better the PA, the less there was for their boss to do. Indeed, secretarial survival demanded enfeebled bosses.

The outward distinctions between PAs often lay in the details. Some had access to arcane computer passwords, reflecting greater trustworthiness. Some had chairs with an ergonomic alignment and desks with private fax machines and room for family photographs. Some of the PAs' work stations resembled schoolgirls' bedrooms housing soft toys, photographs of babies stuck to the side of computers, 'life quotes' cut out from magazines and screen savers from photos taken at office parties.

Jenny Logan's more austere surroundings implied a seriousness about her work. It allowed her to appear steely or playful, depending on the client's financial worth. There was only one picture, an autographed photograph of Olivia Newton John, taped, in a deliberately offhand manner, to a glass partition. It was for others to point out the physical likeness between them. 'Oh, do you think so?' Jenny Logan would say, and she would chuckle with feigned surprise.

Despite this opportunity for banter, there was a touch of stateliness about Jenny's posture, denoting her seniority as well as her commitment to Pilates; her friendliness was tinged with graciousness. She wore suits rather than skirts and tops, maintained an expensive haircut, non-secretarial-length nails and worked long hours. The most visited websites on her computer were the result of research into official business rather than aimless surfing for internet jokes or gossip. Jenny excelled at organizing business trips: finding good (although not ostentatious) central hotels, lining up business-class flights, booking cars. She would make phone calls about computer access, menus, or the proximity of golf courses during her bus ride home at the end of the day, leaning her aching head against the cold, rain-spattered window and then watch her breath cloud up the glass as she interrogated Mid-Western receptionists or Far Eastern officials.

'My life isn't my own!' she would sometimes exclaim in the middle of sorting out her boss's financial entitlements, booking restaurants for his wife or organizing his children's half terms. She meant this positively.

When Richard adjusted his tie, looked out of his office window at the city blinking beneath him and asked her casually what people were saying about the departmental reshuffle/business alliance/marketing strategy/Japanese visitors or asked for suggestions for bring children to work day, he could be sure of Jenny's informed response. The PAs were the company's eyes and ears and much of its brains.

Yet Richard believed they were selectively observant. He thought no one saw him brush against Jenny as he went through his messages. He did not imagine his saucy emails would be intercepted, or that CCTV cameras could record his gropings of her in the lift. Like many bosses he was slow to understand the implications of technology in practice, although in theory he was enthusiastic and visionary. And Jenny, through an act of will, chose not to see her colleagues covert glances or register their sudden silences or read their coded emails. Fridays became her early night.

Jenny had first started working for Richard in December after the hurried departure of his previous secretary. To begin with he had been offhand, almost brusque. He had a patronizing habit of spelling out names to her.

'Yes Mr Wentworth, I know who the head of Microsoft is,' she would say, bristling, her head bent over her notebook.

One day, after dictation, Richard had produced a carrier bag of miscellaneous gifts from under his desk and asked forlornly if she was any good at wrapping.

The Villa

As a matter of fact, wrapping was one of Jenny's talents. She set to work with expensive paper in subdued colours and shredded and twisted ribbon with artistic flourishes. The packages looked as though they came from Madison Avenue.

As she grew to know Richard better she applied the same deftness to their overnight bags and weekend suitcases. She introduced her boss and lover to tissue paper. She slipped sheets of it between his shirts and balls of it into his shoes. Their hotel rooms rustled with its sound and smelt of the perfume Jenny sprayed everywhere with subconscious recklessness. Whatever the human mess of her affair with Richard, it was beautifully packaged.

Jenny did not feel guilty about sleeping with her boss. She said it improved her all-round performance in the office. It made her zestful about getting up in the morning and encouraged her to dress better. She became willing to work as late as necessary and skipped lunch, suddenly self-conscious about what she was eating at her desk and the effect of it on her breath. She felt in a permanent state of readiness. Although doubt was later cast on the basis of her bonuses Jenny knew she honestly deserved them. She would have given blood for the company, so long as it contained Richard.

Jenny particularly treasured the post-coital discussions of meetings and agendas and the derogatory way Richard talked about his colleagues. She, in turn, contributed valuable character insights into those colleagues, based on the secretarial network, even if her examples of greed, thoughtlessness, unhygienic habits and stingy Christmas presents were a year or so out of date.

Jenny never tired of the novelty of seeing Richard with his clothes on and then off. She was unfamiliar with all those inbetween stages that were the province of his wife: silly jumpers, running pants, pyjamas or towels. Jenny only knew him as a modern-day Goliath either in heroic pinstriped armour, or naked and as vulnerable as a piglet. She would run her hand over his chest and peer blissfully at his suit and socks in a heap at the side of the hotel bed. She often considered hiding his clothes so he could not leave. She wanted to lie next to him for ever, his heavy, freckled hand between her thighs the other reaching for his whirring Blackberry on the bedside table.

'We make a good team, don't we darling?' Richard murmured as he rolled away from her.

Jenny took this as a declaration of love and belonging, for it was part of her job to interpret his wishes even before he knew what they were.

After two years of delightful secrecy and make-believe, the revenge of the wives' union was sudden and brutal. Jenny denied the allegations put to her by the head of human resources point blank. Only when the woman said in her slow, neutral voice, 'I have already spoken to Richard,' did Jenny's hand fly to her neck and her knees buckle. Her breathing sounded like a cistern flushing and she looked at the piece of paper pushed across the desk towards her through sun spots of fear. Jenny left the company that afternoon. She was not even allowed to clear her desk or sign off on her computer. When she realized she had left behind her Waitrose shopping bags (containing smoked salmon, ice cream, chocolates and champagne in case Richard came round, and ready-made Caesar salad for one with low-cal dressing, in case he didn't, at a cost of £29.87 in all) she discovered her office entry card refused her access to the building to retrieve them. Her belongings arrived later that afternoon by taxi in two black bin bags. When Richard came round to see her he would not take off his coat, although he did sit down on the nearest chair. He glanced uneasily at the bedroom door and accepted a glass of whisky, gripping it so tightly Jenny feared it would crack. He spoke euphemistically of 'this bloody business' and 'the matter in hand'. Richard's business talent was his power of persuasion. He had come to close the deal. Unfortunately, there was a complication which defeated even Richard's problem-solving skills. Jenny was pregnant.

She would never forget Richard's appalled expression. She

thought he might cry or vomit. He passed his hand over his face and licked his bone-dry lips. They stared at each other like a couple of survivors from a train crash.

The balance of the relationship up to now had been clear: it was Richard who called the shots. He sacrificed independence with every receipt or domestic bill he handed to Jenny, but he still formally issued instructions and she obeyed. Now, for the first time, he faltered. When he asked her, 'And do you want to keep it?' she knew her will would prevail. This was her only chance: she would kick aside the status quo. She saw it as her happiness versus Richard's wife Virginia's. (Later she revised this sentiment upwards to the gift of life versus Virginia's happiness.) And maybe, for a while, Jenny's happiness versus Richard's. You can love *and* blame people, surely? Only war-generation love is free of contradictions.

Jenny felt her voice grow mossy, not with uncertainty but with determination. 'Yes, Richard, I do.'

He coloured, his veins pumping with unpleasant urgency. Jenny felt a surge of anger and tenderness. How did he ever think he could get away with it? She felt very calm. She must be good under pressure. How boss-like! Her inflexibility was strategic: he was going to blink first; the weaker always yield to the stronger; he couldn't find an advantage; he had no negotiating position. Either he had to tell his wife that his mistress was pregnant, in which case she might kick him out, or he had to leave her. Messy and expensive either way. So the question he had to ask himself was this: who would make him feel better about himself? Jenny felt her whole career was a preparation for this moment. She surveyed his miserable face, waxy with sweat, and then she made a cooing sound.

Richard stumbled towards her and took her in his arms. 'I'll do the right thing,' he said, kissing the top of her head with his anaesthetized mouth. 'I'll tell Virginia. Not to worry, Jen. Chin up, old thing.'

She wished he had said he loved her.

Chin up, old thing turned out to be the official position of the Wentworth family, as Jenny discovered when, some time later, Richard drove her to meet his parents at their sixteenth-century Sussex cottage (with river frontage). Of course Jenny had met them before in another context. She had once waited for them at Bank tube station and escorted them to the office in case they lost their way on the five-minute journey. They had seemed to her then shy, elderly, faintly ridiculous. She had fussed over them, issued them with their theatre tickets, fetched them lattes and explained what they were.

Once they were to be her future in-laws the dynamic shifted. The couple were more substantial and alert on their own territory – a low-beamed sitting room with a pink carpet and some decent antiques. Richard's mother served China tea and cakes, smoothed her skirt and surveyed Jenny with bright blue triangular-shaped eyes. Richard's father sat on the other side of the room in his worn leather armchair and lowered his spectacles onto his beaky nose. The conversation was studiedly impersonal: planning issues in the village, the effect of the rain on the garden, the welfare of the queen.

'I can't believe they never mentioned the baby. They didn't even ask about the wedding,' Jenny blurted out on the journey home, fishing inside her handbag for a scented tissue. 'Are they actually aware we are going to get married?'

Richard glanced in his rear mirror and signalled as he moved into the outside lane. He sniffed and opened his window a crack. Jenny's perfume had become oppressive. The only sound was the screeching windscreen wipers on the misted window and Jenny's snivelling. Outside was a drizzling dusk.

'Of course they are,' he said evenly.

'Oh, are they? And how can you tell?' said Jenny, manoeuvring her voluptuous stomach so she could examine his heavy profile with the boxer's nose and hard mouth. It was a face that softened in passion, but which was non-negotiable in business. She felt like one of the Japanese visitors. Her nose was running again. She wiped it with her hand.

'Because my parents had removed the photographs of Virginia and Toby from the mantelpiece. They were in the kitchen,' said Richard. 'Those wipers need replacing. Does the noise irritate you?'

'Chin up, old thing,' Richard said again as he examined the hotel menu while waiting for his son Toby to join them for tea. It was the same hotel they had used for post-lunch love making, or afternoon conferences as they were called at the office. To be honest, Jenny had found some of those spontaneous sex sessions contrived. They both made too many noises: 'Mmmmm', as they kissed; over-emphatic expletives when they made love to disguise the fact that their glands could not match their cerebral expectations of an office fling. Jenny's lust relied on the slow foreplay of the office day: Richard's hand on hers as she passed him his morning coffee, his breath on her neck as he ran through some paperwork, his glance at his watch in the early evening and his offer to run her home via a bar near her street. The truth was that comfort on expenses did not produce the highest-quality sex. Richard was better when he fucked her on the front seat of the car outside her flat.

Richard and Jenny did not allude to their previous visits to the hotel. It would not have been tasteful to muse about gymnastic positions in the lift in a location chosen for its proximity to Toby's school. A month ago, they had staggered somewhat drunkenly into the hotel lobby. Now they sat primly in dainty chairs and murmured to each other about the decor like a couple of maiden aunts.

Toby approached with uncertain steps, laden with gym bags and a violin case. He had a cap of thick springy hair, huge grey-brown eyes, sloping shoulders and grey flannel trousers which stopped short of his ankles.

'Ah, Toby,' said Richard standing up. 'You know Jenny. Come and say hello.'

Well, yes, they did know each other – Toby had visited the office a few times – although he seemed to have grown six inches in as many months. Jenny had hugged him and swivelled him round in Richard's office chair, given him paper and crayons, put bags of sweets into his pockets. When Richard brought him in for fathers and children day she had taken him to have his face painted and had comforted him when he was poked in the eye with the paintbrush. His tiger face had been smeared by stinging tears. But now she was no longer Daddy's PA, she was Daddy's special friend. Daddy's pregnant special friend.

Toby put out his hand to shake, his eyes lowered beneath spider-leg eyelashes. Then he sat down, placed his hands on his knees in an impression of manliness and looked around the restaurant, stared at the tea menu, blinked at the overhead light – anything not to meet Jenny's eye.

*

The wedding was a challenge for Jenny. Naturally she suggested to Richard that something quiet and quick would be most appropriate. Of course, what she had in mind was a cathedral, a Christmas-card choir and a bridal train that snaked across ancient flagstones. Her favourite film was *The Sound of Music*, that fairy-tale victory for employees.

Richard applauded her common sense, ignoring the cries of her heart. He booked a convenient town hall. Jenny knew from years of professional training not to contradict the boss. Better to insinuate an alternative, park it and leave it there, until your boss believes it's his own idea. Jenny fathomed that Richard had two weak points: money and Toby. God forgive her, but Jenny used both.

'I wonder if it would be fun for Toby if we made the wedding part of a little holiday? Just the three of us. An all inclusive to St Lucia.'

Richard was living in Jenny's two-bedroom flat at the time. One bedroom was his study. Instinctively, she started sorting his solicitor's bills into the in and out trays.

Richard's face brightened at the mention of Toby but frowned over the potential expense.

'St Lucia is for footballers, darling. Couldn't you find somewhere a bit cheaper?'

Jenny wound a new roll of paper into the fax machine.

'Oh, this is very cheap. My mum can get the air tickets,

business class on discount so long as we go via Frankfurt, and it's off season. I'll need to book it today, though.'

The fact that Jenny's mother was a former air hostess had once tickled Richard's lust. He had whispered to Jenny that he would like to see her in a British Airways outfit. Jenny had debated whether to purchase the unflattering suit but decided that fantasies rarely translated into reality. As a compromise, she had arrived at work in a vibrant red two-piece with matching lipstick and high heels. 'Just like a Virgin!' she murmured to Richard as she brought him his first coffee of the day. He had looked puzzled, although he fucked her with renewed vigour that night.

They had arrived in St Lucia after a sixteen-hour flight and booked into a hotel packed with Sunday footballers. The schedule for weddings was tight – one every twenty minutes. Their slot was midday, by which time the temperature was in the high thirties and Toby had started to throw up from exhaustion. The gold-embossed photograph, which was part of the holiday package, showed Jenny and Richard in front of a steel band and Toby a blur at the corner as he raced to the toilet. Richard was cascading sweat and Jenny's fresh white cotton dress drooped, like a lily without water, over her distended belly. It was not a photograph to be framed, reprinted or passed around the office.

The Villa

The honeymoon night was memorable for the foul heat, noise and smell. Jenny could not open the window, which was above the hotel dustbins, without being assaulted by mosquitoes. The fan was as loud as a jet engine. Richard went to sleep in the bath. So Jenny lay next to Toby, his open eyes like rock pools, and stroked his wringing wet hair and told him the story of Christopher Columbus and other great adventurers. From time to time, he would wriggle closer to her, his unflavoured breath on her ear, his hand curling into hers.

'I still can't get to sleep,' he whispered, with a hint of panic.

"I know; it doesn't matter. Isn't it funny being so far away from home with the sea just outside. Shall we go on more holidays together?'

'Only if we can have air conditioning,' Toby joked, with a sob.

'Oh, we will. Now Daddy and I are married everything will be different. We're all going to have such fun together.'

There was a whoop and rattle at the window, followed by the hiss of rain. Toby's breath was even, punctuated by little sighs and hiccoughs. His head bore down painfully on her chest, leaving a red imprint by the morning.

Jenny's wedding gave her at least provisional, off-peak membership of the wives' union. The birth of her daughter Emily three months later bestowed new rights. Chief of these was the right to revisit the office. She chose her moment carefully, a Friday afternoon when everyone would still be present but not over-occupied. She breastfed Emily in the car park, before unwrapping the tissue paper around the tiny checked seer-sucker dress and popping the matching cotton cap over the baby's warm head. Jenny hugged Emily to her shoulder and joined the ants-in-trouser-suits procession of workers across the mall to the central reception area. She thought about picking up a coffee, but the risk of spillage was too great and she no longer had enough hands. Jenny smiled at the familiar receptionist, who looked back at her blankly.

'Can I help you?'

'Yes, I have come to see my husband, Richard Wentworth. Extension 802.'

The ensemble of maternal sexiness she had created unravelled as Emily's arm shot out and yanked the sunglasses from her head. They dropped to the floor Jenny squatted down and felt for them. Emily belched curdled milk over her mother's hair and jacket.

'Go right up,' said the receptionist.

There was no one to meet her as she came out of the lift. Once, she had a card to get her through the office doors. Now, she was forced to tap on the glass, peering at her old colleagues in front of their computers. Colleen, her closest friend, was emptying the contents of a Boots bag onto her desk, giving a running commentary that evoked gusts of silent laughter around her. Jenny tapped harder. Colleen turned round, shook her head with surprise and slowly rose from her seat. Jenny thought she was going to pass right by her, but she opened the doors and gave a gratifying scream at the sight of Emily.

'Oh, will you look at that! She's teeeny! Look at her!'

Jenny held her trophy aloft, limbs swinging.

A small crowd gathered around her.

'What is she called?'

'How much does she weigh?'

'Those tiny hands. She's opening her eyes, look.'

'What colour are her eyes?'

'Can I hold her?'

It was as Jenny had mentally rehearsed it. Apart from dribbling curds, Emily behaved with grace. Jenny was the centre of attention again, but this time through maternal virtue rather than scandal. A plump, pretty woman whom Jenny had not seen before peered over Colleen's shoulder.

'Whose baby, where's the baby?' she asked.

'It's Mrs Wentworth,' said Colleen formally. 'Richard's wife.'

How ordinary and strange the description sounded to Jenny. She smiled and held out her hand, clutching Emily to her with her other arm and her chin.

'Oh, hello. I'm Irene, I've heard so much about you. Richard told me how you could have been a concert pianist. I love the piano too.'

Jenny's heart descended like a lift. She gripped Emily's light form and kissed her head frantically.

'Is this Toby?' continued Irene, radiant with good will. 'I must have misunderstood; I thought he was much older.'

Colleen held up her hand like a policeman trying to control traffic at a rogue traffic light. 'Stop right there, Irene,' she said with force and humour. 'You have the wrong Mrs Wentworth. This is the second Mrs Wentworth.'

Irene's face shrunk like a deflated balloon.

'Oh, goodness! I am sorry.'

Jenny jigged up and down with relentless cheerfulness. Emily released another stream of milk in response.

'There, there. That's better. Not to worry, easily done.'

At that moment, Richard emerged from his office and took in the gathering with a wide-screen gaze.

'Jenny. Emily. Darling!' he said courteously taking Jenny's arm and guiding her to the lift doors. 'How good of you to come. Do you have the car downstairs? Why don't you go and wait for me there and I'll join you in a minute.'

Colleen stood back, her head lowered. As Jenny was whisked through the doors, she heard her old pals weakly wish her goodbye. This was not right; she had caused a scene. She kissed Richard on the cheek and watched the lift doors close through a smear of tears. Emily was starting to struggle and whimper. Office workers on their way home poured into the lift at each floor until Jenny was crushed against the side. Emily belted out a warning cry. Men and women in indistinguishable suits glanced at Jenny curiously and turned away. She felt hot and intimidated. For God's sake, she had a right to be there. Mothers were people too. Emily banged her head against Jenny's chest and her mouth opened wide and wavered as in a cartoon, 'Whaaaaaaaaaah.'

The suits pretended not to notice the glass-shattering noise, being trained to deal with unusual disturbance. In the face of hysteria, anger or breakdown you kept calm and waited for security. A guard stepped forward at reception and asked Jenny if she needed assistance.

'It's just a baby!' screamed Jenny. 'What's the matter with you all?' She pushed her way through the revolving doors and ran to the car park.

As she sat in heightened misery, breastfeeding Emily in the passenger seat, she saw Richard casually striding towards her, his footsteps echoing on the concrete. He opened the back door and placed his briefcase on the seat. Then he opened the driver's door and pushed back the seat. He sat down and held the steering wheel with stiff arms.

'OK?' he said, looking ahead.

Jenny buttoned up her blouse and put on her seat belt. Sexual disarray was one thing but breastfeeding was another.

'I am so, so sorry,' she said flatly.

'You've nothing to be sorry for,' said Richard, patting her hand. His forgiveness formalized her offence. Jenny had tried to get a foothold in two camps, but she had no place in the office and was still on trial at home. She was in no man's land.

'I just want a place where I can be myself,' she said.

'Of course,' said Richard, retuning the radio.

'I need you away from work and away from home. That's where we are happy,' Jenny added despairingly.

'Like where?' asked Richard.

'Just somewhere else. Like on holiday. We can relax then. Be ourselves. I just feel . . .'

'What?'

'That I need a new context.'

Two

Ten Years Later

The package flopped through the letterbox onto the polished French oak floor of Jenny Wentworth's substantial Chiswick home. She judged the weight of the thud from her conservatory kitchen and clenched her left fist with pleasure. That was not a catalogue thud, which sounded flimsier and acoustically softened by its polythene wrapper. It was not the whisper of a school prospectus or Richard's share portfolios. No, it was the lovely thump of the latest holiday brochure, thick as a book and with better illustrations.

'That's the post,' said Jenny casually as she carried the kettle to its base, pressed the switch to red and squeezed past Richard's intimidating form. The kitchen had been extended twice but two people could still not comfortably pass each other at the central island where Richard noisily munched his toast.

'I'll get it on my way out,' he said, exhaling Marmite breath.

'No, darling, you must keep still while you eat. You'll get heartburn.'

'Don't fuss over me,' said Richard. 'And where have you put my briefcase?'

Jenny smiled with determined gaiety.

'I'm getting mixed messages, darling. It's my job to look after you.'

She bent to pick up the case from the pile of coats that had fallen from a mean wall hook.

'Perhaps when you have time . . .'

Richard grabbed the case, trapping Jenny's fingers in the handle. 'I don't have time. I am working too damn hard to pay for everything here.'

Jenny put her arm behind her back. Her husband was not at his best in the mornings. She would compensate with exaggerated cheerfulness.

'Of course, dear.' She beamed at him, turned and floated towards the hallway, then ran, her dressing gown flapping open, revealing wide-apart breasts and a protruding stomach (a flaw which drove her, after consideration and regret, from bikini to one-piece). She grabbed the brochure, glanced furtively behind her and, opening a door to her right, threw the package into the drawing room. Then she closed the door and picked up the rest of the envelopes which she carried back, like a Labrador, to her husband.

'More bloody bills,' said Richard frowning at her. She could not think why. Jenny sighed sympathetically.

'Right, I'm off.'

'Have your cup of tea first.'

'No, I'm off.'

Jenny followed her husband to the front door. At the top of the stairs a sprite-like figure appeared with tousled hair and wearing pink pants.

'Are you going, Daddy?' said the child, hesitating before she noiselessly started down the steps.

'Emily, get dressed. You can't come down like that,' said Jenny with her arms folded.

'I want to say goodbye to Daddy,' said Emily, her toes curling over the edge of each stair as she descended further.

'Go back upstairs and get dressed,' said Jenny with, she felt, the correct degree of humour and firmness.

Richard opened the front door.

'Have a good day at school, darling,' he said over his shoulder. 'Do as Mummy says.'

The door slammed behind him.

Emily's jaw shot forward like a ledge and she turned proudly on her heel. Jenny watched her stalk back up the stairs, her bobbing spine visible in her slender back, her winter tan forming the shape of her swimming costume.

'You can do some piano practice if you like,' called Jenny, in what she would have described as a sing-song voice.

'No,' Emily called back coldly. 'You told me to get dressed. I'm getting dressed.'

Jenny sighed. Why did everyone have to be so cross with her? Had she ever raised her voice? Did she behave unreasonably? Of course not. She had smiled and coaxed her way through adult life. Richard had appreciated her solicitous little touches when she was his secretary: the way she arranged his flowers, took dictation and opened her blouse for him to have a quick squeeze when he was under pressure. Oh yes, he had liked having her around then. He would bellow 'Jenny!' from his office, and she would leap up from her desk and come running.

There was a crash above her, followed by a wail. Emily's drawer. Jenny had told her not to hang on to it; she had told her. The mahogany was warped by the central heating. Oh, this was trying.

'Coming, darling!' she chimed as she tripped up the superior-quality stair carpet. Emily was crouched on the floor surrounded by T-shirts, light sweaters from the Boden spring collection and limbless dolls arranged in Chapman Brother-style symbolic piles of destitution and suffering. Emily's indignant face was warm and damp and she was sucking her index finger.

'I've got a splinter.' She hiccoughed.

'Let me have a look,' said Jenny, bending down next to her, feeling the rapid fluttering breaths through Emily's ribcage.

The Villa

Emily insisted on holding her finger up in the air in the back of the car on the journey to school.

'Emily, I can't see if you do that. You can put your finger down,' said Jenny, turning round. A van hooted and swerved. Jenny gave a little wave and mouthed sorry. The driver mimed an expletive in response.

She remembered the time Richard had gone to pick up a sleek new company car and she had accompanied him to the garage in order to help with the paperwork and to share his high spirits. The seats were low and wide, making a little fellatio en route back to the office quite comfortable. Nobody had hooted at them then, although Jenny had been committing a far more serious traffic offence. The harder she tried to be good, the more irritated everyone became with her. Family life was like the inside of Emily's piano – taut-wired and mysteriously intricate. She needed to create a more relaxing, enjoyable environment. A holiday environment.

She straightened at the prospect. Her yoga teacher had taught her that in order to be calm, one had to clear one's mind of petty, everyday fears. One had to imagine white sand and a clear, pale blue sea lapping around one's feet. Jenny could not remember if her teacher had mentioned a hotel waiter advancing towards her with cocktails decorated with tiny umbrellas and club sandwiches. This was probably too detailed for elementary meditation, but it was how Jenny liked to picture the scene.

She loaded Emily with gym bag and homework case and watched her melt into a crowd of small people in blazers and white socks, finger still pointing skyward like a fourteenth-century religious painting. She wanted to run after her and hug her, but the headmistress discouraged guilt and hysteria among school-run mothers. Jenny wished for the pre-school days; love felt in hindsight is always the strongest.

She sighed, turned on the ignition and swung into the middle of the road as if she were driving an articulated lorry rather than a standard Cherokee jeep. She parked over two spaces outside the house and jumped out, wrapping her coat over her tracksuit. The gym was usually her next stop, but she had remembered that Rosa the cleaner was coming early and to be honest she could do with some non-judgmental company. What are staff if not a professionalization of friendship? A dinner party of choice would include her builder, her cleaner and the man on the third till at Waitrose. These were the people who knew and appreciated her *for herself.* The third-till man particularly. 'Why, you've bought mangoes today, that's unlike you. It's usually kiwi fruit, am I right? Have you got an account with us?' Usually he was not right, but it was so thoughtful of him to try to understand her. Retail psychology almost moved her to tears. All those computers and credit-card companies anticipating her impulse buys, her likes and dislikes, the geography of her life, her moods. So sweet. A filing system for humanity. Who else was interested in her?

The Villa

Jenny liked watching order spread through the house in separate phases: the kitchen swept and washed; the taps polished; cloths hung neatly to dry. Today it was the turn of the ground floor and she heard the sound of the Hoover, like a plane taking off, in the drawing room. The Hoover needed fixing but she did not want to trouble Richard with it. Jenny had looked at a few advertisements in *Yellow Pages* but when she phoned the numbers there was always an answering machine and she was often uncertain about the post codes. What if, when she finally found the place, it was closed? Domestic tasks such as these were so much easier to achieve in an office. Business to business. At home it was one echoing phone to another. And when you did get hold of someone they were so careless with your custom. Even door-to-door salesmen looked over your shoulder and asked when your husband would be home. It was imperative to give a different daytime and evening telephone number. Unless, of course, you were American.

Jenny sighed again. In a way, she would prefer the Hoover to pack up altogether so she could buy a new one. But for now it struggled on deafeningly, picking up threads and coins but leaving semi-invisible debris.

'Hi, Rosa,' she shouted, poking her blonde, jauntily bobbed hair round the door. 'I'm back.'

Rosa switched off the machine and stood to attention. She was a tiny woman, with a coil of thick black hair round her wide-nosed, pock-marked face. Jenny gave her Emily's cast-off clothes, so today Rosa was wearing a Boden cotton sweater emblazoned with a purple star, flared lilac trousers and trainers which lit up when she moved. Despite her doll-like frame, she supported a family of eight back in the Philippines as well as her aged parents. Jenny did not altogether grasp economic migration. Her last cleaner had come from Tobago and Jenny could never understand why. There were such lovely beaches in Tobago – surely it was better to live off coconuts than slum it in a bedsit in Acton. But there was no real holiday dimension to the Philippines; you were probably better off in Chiswick.

She was aware that Rosa helped herself to coins lying around the house, but this, in Jenny's estimation, was a fair distribution of wealth. Everybody needed a little holiday-money.

'How was Emily this morning?' asked Rosa, rubbing the back of her neck. Jenny was so grateful for her concern. When other people asked about her daughter she knew it was only out of politeness. For example, when Richard's friends said with bored respect, 'And are you a full-time mum, Jenny?'

'Poor Emily. The wretched drawer fell in her bedroom again and she got a splinter in her finger. She was shaking like a leaf when I pulled it out. I couldn't get her to stay still. Ah, well, she'll survive.'

'She's a survivor,' Rosa nodded gravely. 'This your brochure? It was on the floor.'

Jenny flushed. 'Oh, is that what it is? It's so important for Richard to get some rest; he works so hard. I'm wondering about the south of France this summer.'

'Very nice,' said Rosa. 'By the sea?'

'Well, I'd like a sea view. We don't actually need to go in the sea. European beaches aren't terribly clean. I'm thinking about a villa with a pool. Nothing too grand, I have to look after the purse strings. Otherwise Richard will come and rationalize the household. He might want to sack Emily for not pulling her weight. Ha ha – only joking.'

'Can I look?' asked Rosa, her sweet smile rolling like a wave across her face.

Jenny hesitated, then tore off the brown paper. The brochure had a matt Tiffany-blue cover and silver embossed writing. The company was called Premier Villas. Jenny, who was five foot seven, bent down to share the brochure with Rosa as if it were a hymn book. Some of the villas were too large, some too small, some too secluded, some too open. One had to learn to read between the lines. You would not buy a house without checking whether there was a brick factory or main road near by. Yet people booked holidays on the strength of one photograph and a piece of advertising copy. They were careful about residency but risked recuperation, that precious exaltation of being. No wonder there were such terrible disappointments. Why, only that week Jenny had read of a woman who had booked a villa in Barbados to celebrate the millennium.

She had paid over £30,000 for it and discovered that the rooms were dark and the breakfast cups too small. When the woman won her civil suit against the holiday company there was a tone of derision in the newspapers – complained about the breakfast cups! Jenny did not laugh. The delicate balance between contentment and disappointment could easily rest in a breakfast cup. It is terribly difficult to arrange life harmoniously. The component parts are too complex. But for a few weeks a year one had a shot at it. Jenny prided herself that she had become more than a holiday maker, she was a connoisseur of holidays. She had the knowledge of a travel editor, so when Richard's boss mentioned she was travelling to the Seychelles Jenny raised her eyebrow and asked 'North island?' Oh yes, she could tell the difference. The world's beaches were of boundless interest to her.

She was not a tourist or a traveller, she was a holiday buff. The foreign pages of newspapers were a mystery to her, but she avidly read the holiday dramas on page three as if the speed-boat accidents, jeep crashes and ambushes were family events. Her library of brochures and photograph albums was her life's work.

Jenny pointed to the penultimate page of the brochure, a villa situated on a hill of lavender, modernized but traditional, with a tennis court and a large pool.

'But is it too far away from the sea?' she asked anxiously, her baby-pink polished nail moving across the description.

'In the corner, over the hill. The blue bit. That's the sea, I think,' said Rosa excitedly.

Jenny took a breath. 'You're right, Rosa. I think we have found the perfect villa.'

Holidays were the best part of Jenny's marriage to Richard. They imitated some of the ingredients of their affair: the cocktails, the lack of responsibility, the desire for sex. Holidays had the same rhythm as an affair – anticipation (the more prolonged the better), snatched moments, a sense of time running out, regret and relief, memories. The thrill of discovery and possibility matched by a certainty that you would not want to stay permanently.

Had marriage been a mistake? No, no, of course not. Hedonism is a finite condition, one has to settle.

Jenny did not like to go too deeply into the circumstances of their marriage. Elapsed time had taken the sting out of it. Only when new friends asked brightly, 'So, tell me, how did you two meet?' did Jenny feel the prickle, the twinge, the discomfort. Like an old injury. Her romantic narrative was always going to be caught up in somebody else's tragedy.

Richard's first wife Virginia had been pretty decent about it, really. Since the women spoke often, sharing jokes about Richard's obsession with punctuality and his hopelessness about buying presents, it had been more of a transfer than a divorce. Jenny told herself and then others, fixing her eyes on them to check whether they frowned or jerked their heads in disagreement, that Virginia must have been out of love with her husband to relinquish him. But she had her doubts. She had observed a kind of proud fatalism in Virginia. Perhaps it was to do with not working. Jenny had been indoctrinated with the business principle that you do not take no for an answer. Virginia was like the sea, pulling those she loved towards her and then repelling them. Despite her marital vows she had no sense of possession, whereas Jenny had an outsider's need for ownership. She admired Virginia for releasing her husband from their life together, and also despised her for her yielding nature. Virginia ended up valuing Richard's happiness above her own. Frankly, Jenny explained to third parties, she had been a lousy wife.

Jenny was also disappointed in the alteration to her relationship with Virginia. Part of the delight and rhythm of her affair with Richard lay in the conversations that she had had with his wife. They had had an intimacy based on betrayal. Jenny missed the exchange of information, the insights, Virginia's slow, easy speech and nicotine laugh. (How Richard complained about Virginia's smoking. How Jenny acted on it, with her own peppermint puritanism.) She missed the family photographs on Richard's office desk: Virginia looking sideways at the camera, with caustic dark eyes and a slightly hooked nose, her black hair cascading down her back; Virginia on a Norfolk beach with Toby squinting at their sandcastle with shy pride. Jenny had since avoided English holidays. Out of taste.

Was that partly why her holiday snaps screamed Second Wife?

She shook herself. No point in dwelling on the past; it was all just photos in scrapbooks now.

'You gonna book it?' asked Rosa shyly.

'I'll need to do some research,' said Jenny, in the manner of a nuclear scientist. 'You can't rush these things. You've got to get them right.'

Rosa whistled softly. 'You have to look into it. You want me to do some ironing today?'

Jenny thought. 'No, there are five shirts left in Richard's wardrobe. Do the ironing on Thursday. That's best.'

She suddenly wanted to hug Rosa, but this would alter their relationship irrevocably. Cleaners discouraged desperate intimacy and tearful affection.

So Jenny embarked on her project. Builders and holidays were her preserve in the house. OK, it wasn't the stock exchange. Let others mock, let their eyes glaze over, but one could not be slipshod; it required meticulous planning. Men fixed on professional goals and women on continual self-improvement.

Her mouth stretched into a peculiar grimace while she was

thinking. Since Jenny had been married she had developed several mildly compulsive habits: she had to close every door in the house; she performed a three-part sequence of glancing from her hands, to her feet, to her chest until her eyes felt strained; she gave little rictus grins. This had only happened once in company, when she was juggling saucepans with her back to her guests. Richard had, unusually, wandered over to help.

'What are you doing with your mouth?' he had asked with a laugh that suggested repugnance.

Jenny had jumped. 'Oh, my lips are chapped. Sorry, sorry.'

As she sat in front of the internet, browsing through the hundreds of holiday sites and their links, all listed as 'favourites', she stretched her mouth at twenty-second intervals. Richard's friends would have scoffed, but she could assure them it was a morning's work. Ask any secretary.

Jenny's rolling project of holidays was seasonally at odds. Even as she was packing Emily's anorak, socks and glasses for skiing, her mind was on the warmth ahead. In the summer, she thought about the winter. She tried to contain her enthusiastic long-term forecasts because they irritated Richard, but sometimes they slipped out. As he lowered himself onto a deckchair in loudly patterned swimming trunks, she might say dreamily, 'I think the hotel is going to be better located in the Seychelles,' or, 'I can't decide whether we need to hire a car for Lake Garda.'

'Can't you just enjoy yourself and stop thinking where you are dragging us off to next?' Richard would frown, pull the elastic of his trunks up over his thickening stomach and hold a paperback up to his face. (Always the same book, *The Day of the Jackal.* He said that he'd enjoyed it before, so would enjoy it again. No point in wasting money on alternative plots.)

To be frank, Richard was no more sensitive to his environment than he was to reading. One beach was the same as the next. Once his shoulders were burnt red and he had performed some lengths of splashy, water-displacing crawl he was ready to go home.

Whereas to Jenny every grain of sand was different. Every beach had to be explored. Within reason. Since 11 September 2001, her holiday map of the world had shrunk alarmingly. Africa was reduced to its southern tip. Central Asia was plunged into oblivion. Bali had been a terrible wrench. She reserved judgement on Australia. Scandinavia had shot up her list. Secretly, she admired France for its refusal to go to war in Iraq. Tourists slept safely in their hotel beds as a result.

In a way, Richard was right: the holidays were most potent to her before or after they took place. The first day was always a let down (she returned to her sexual analogy). Only by the third day could she judge whether the holiday was a success. Only afterwards could she confidently pronounce that she had enjoyed it. Interestingly, obvious catastrophes, such as illness, were not always obstacles. A trip to the hospital could provide a shared anecdote and more emphatic memory, so long as no one died. Obviously. No, the failures were more to do with a lack of holiday spirit, a refusal to gel. Holidays that were a mere extension of home life.

She heard the front door slam shut. That would be Rosa, heavens it must be midday already. (Rosa was paid to do four hours, so naturally she left after three. That seemed reasonable to Jenny, who was more open about the wasted hours in a working day than Richard's corporate amour propre would allow.)

Jenny would pop out herself soon to fetch the ingredients for a soften-Richard-up dinner and her own Deli soup. Richard never asked her what she ate for lunch although she always questioned him about his in fascinated detail. The enormous contrast between his Savoy Grill courses and her secretarial/pensioner nibbling used to make Jenny feel virtuous, but since the shake-up instigated by Richard's new woman boss he had become plaintive about his meagre sandwich at his desk. Jenny encouraged him to bitch about Darcy Rumbelow, but she was secretly grateful that some of the joie de vivre had disappeared from the office. It made her feel safer.

She rubbed her eyes lightly to avoid wrinkles. It was over ten years since Richard had last told her she looked like Olivia Newton John. She used to collect magazines that featured the singer, scattering them round the house to invite comparison. She had even pinned a picture of Olivia up in the study, on the pretext of needing a recipe on the other side of the page. Over the years the picture had become mysteriously water-marked and stained. There were no newer pictures with which to replace it. Olivia had faded from public consciousness as had Jenny in her smaller way.

When Jenny gave up work she had grand plans for the empty expanse of days before her. Her horizons were as vast as the ocean. But apart from her projects and her pottery class she could not remember further achievements. The school day was so much shorter than the office day. Furthermore, because Jenny often missed the first days of term which had not always coincided with her holiday dates, she had never mastered the rota of play dates and clubs and coffee mornings. She hung back at the school gates on the edges of groups, smiling appealingly. But no one addressed or included her, and she was too shy to break into the conversation. Why? Jenny had never been shy when she worked in an office. Maybe because there were always procedures to follow, assigned roles for everybody, gifts, such as new fax rolls or Post-it messages to offer. Jenny was Richard's secretary, which was somehow more tangible than being Richard's second wife.

She had not expected it to be difficult to form relationships with the other mothers. But they all found firm friends early and stuck to them, just as their children did. Jenny seemed to make an odd number: the one too many for any game or conversation or dinner party. She feared she was suspected of being a single mother, since Richard never managed to go to parent and teacher evenings. The only time she made friends was on holiday.

Arriving at school to collect her daughter, Jenny thought yet again how she envied Emily her self-assurance and easy popularity. Emily sought out her mother with the same small Caribbean-blue-coloured eyes as her father had, and sauntered towards her, waving away her friends.

'Bye, Emily,' 'See you, Emily,' 'Hey, Emily. Bye,' they chorused. The other mothers put out hands to Emily as she passed them. She gave her mother a rueful, pitying smile and put her hand into hers. Her daughter's fingers were like chicken wishbones, so small they could snap. Jenny's eyes filled with tears.

'How was your day?' she asked as she held open the passenger door.

'OK,' said Emily, settling herself in the front seat and putting on her seat belt. 'I came third in the spelling test.'

'Did you, darling? Third. That's fantastic.'

'It's OK, it's not fantastic,' said Emily looking out of the window. 'It would have been fantastic if I had come first.'

That was Richard speaking. Jenny marvelled at the strength of his influence on a daughter he barely saw, whereas her outwardly conciliatory and fretful nature hardly made an imprint on Emily, despite a good four hours of quality time per day. She supposed this was a result of her weaker genes.

Once they got home, Emily skipped up the stairs humming to herself and shut her bedroom door behind her. Without explanation. When called for tea, she reappeared in a halter-neck top and hipsters, which Jenny only allowed inside the house and was secretly planning to donate to Rosa.

Jenny sat opposite her daughter at the table, toying with a plate containing a piece of pizza and a pile of ready-washed salad. Emily chewed at hers, eyeing her mother. Jenny smiled encouragingly. In her head she was calculating which sauce to serve with Richard's chicken – lemon? mushroom and cream? – and how to broach the holiday question. She shook herself. Minutes had passed without the pair exchanging a word.

'So, what did you have for lunch?' she asked leaning forward on her elbows.

Emily sighed. 'It's not interesting, Mummy.'

That was the trouble. The things that interested Jenny bored the rest of her family. She never imagined that a nine-year-old girl would be such a difficult conversationalist. She looked at the inscrutable miniature face before her with rising panic.

'I'm thinking of booking a holiday in France,' she said. 'Would you like to speak French?'

Emily frowned. 'Why do we have to go away? I like it here. My things are here.'

'Holidays are always nice. You want to have adventures, don't you?'

'Yeah. S'pose.' Emily shrugged. 'Can I watch telly now?'

Jenny picked up her plate with relief.

'Yes, if you have finished your homework. Half an hour until I run your bath.'

Was summer pudding the right choice for February? It might get Richard in the mood. Otherwise there was cheese; she should take that out of the fridge now. Or fruit. She would use Emily's bath water, it would save time. Was the clock fast? That was the marvellous thing about holidays. All food preparation time became relaxation.

The telephone purred on the wall. Jenny blinked at it with a quiet dread. What if it were the parent of one of Emily's classmates or a colleague of Richard's with demands she could not meet or asking for information she did not have. The sound of the phone in this period of warm, brightly lit domestic activity was an act of aggression.

'Phone,' said Emily, not taking her eyes from the television.

'Why don't you get it, Emily?' said Jenny, tiptoeing to the far side of the kitchen. 'I'm just in the middle of something.'

Emily gave a loud sigh and pulled at the phone, stretching the wire round the corner so she could still see the television.

'Hey. Oh, hi. I'm OK. I'm watching TV. No, it's a new episode.'

Jenny hovered by her mixing bowls trying to catch Emily's eye.

'Mum's here, but she's in the middle of something.'

Jenny waved her arms.

'Who is it?' she mimed.

Emily raised her eyebrows.

'It's Toby,' she said flatly into the phone.

Jenny grabbed at it.

'Give it to me. Sorry, Toby, here I am. Sorry.'

Toby was a friendly presence in an increasingly bewildering world. It was the strangest thing. The person who had most reason to dislike Jenny, who had lost his father and his security because of her, showed her the greatest sympathy. Whenever Jenny reflected on this paradox she felt tears spill from the corners of her eyes.

Toby had bypassed adolescence, changing from a polite formal child to a considerate easy-going young adult. His eighteenth birthday had been one of the nicest parties Jenny had ever been to. Toby combined the best features of his parents, but most of all he was himself. He was a triumph of nature.

They always found plenty to talk about. Jenny was interested in his education, but she had come into her own on the subject of his gap year. True, he preferred travel to holidays, but the distinction was a point of friendly banter. He had once insisted she accompany him parasailing above the Indian

Ocean. Jenny had been frightened inside her baby harness and had refused to open her eyes.

'You don't know what you're missing!' Toby had laughed into the wind as they danced above the disappearing raft. 'You can see everything from up here!'

Jenny hadn't wanted to see everything. She had wanted the safe confinement of a beach and a chaise longue. She had whimpered in terror.

'You're perfectly safe. I'm right here. I'll look after you,' Toby had called out and, opening one eye, she could indeed see his long-limbed frame and flying dark hair. She stopped mewling and felt less giddy and inside out. Toby was there. Her step-son and her friend.

'Oh, Toby, how nice to hear from you. I'm doing chicken tonight, won't you come round? You've eaten? What a pity. I need some moral support. OK, OK, not exactly moral. I've found this wonderful place in the South of France. I had an idea that lots of us could go, some of our friends, you, Emily. I thought it would be so great for us all to be together. I'm happy to cook. What do you think?'

Emily was watching, her head on one side, legs crossed as if in assembly. Jenny laughed and twisted the phone wire round her finger. She shifted her weight onto one foot, then ran her hand through her hair and laughed again. Her face became rosy with animation. She put down the phone and winked at Emily. She stepped towards her and gave her a playful shove. Emily grunted in mock irritation, trying not to smile. Jenny started to tickle her.

'No, Mummy, no! Don't do that.' Jenny rolled her over and Emily laughed cavernously.

'We're going on holiday, holiday, holiday,' sang Jenny as her daughter flailed beneath her.

'OK, we're going on holiday,' gasped Emily.

Neither heard the front door open and shut or the purposeful tread of hand-made shoes on the floor. Moments later a boulder in a black coat stopped in front of them.

'Oh, darling,' said Jenny, jumping up. Emily rolled over and stretched out her legs wide apart.

'So we're going on holiday?' said Richard in the rumbling voice that Jenny had loved in the office and feared at home.

'We were just fooling around. Heavens, you're early: I must go and put some make-up on and get dressed.'

'Yes, I suppose it is time to get up,' said Richard taking off his coat. His black hair, now beginning to go grey, had a set look to it. Are people chosen for their jobs because they look the part or do they come to look like their jobs?

While Jenny fluttered around her husband, taking his coat, pouring him a glass of wine, lighting the hob, Emily lay back with her hands behind her head, as relaxed as a sunbather. She did not fear her father one bit.

'So how come you're early?' She yawned, her mouth cat pink. 'Did you get the sack?'

'No, Emily. Sorry to disappoint you,' said Richard lowering himself onto the armchair and hitching his trousers up at the knees so that an inch of white flesh showed above his black socks. 'I had meetings in town. How was ballet?'

Jenny noted, without bitterness, that despite the paucity of landmarks in her and Emily's week, Richard was incapable of remembering them. Ballet was Wednesday, Jenny's pottery class was Thursday. Not too complicated and quite unvarying. Richard was not to blame, he had never understood Jenny's filing system which she continued to carry in her head. It was the greatest power she had over him.

She wondered how his replacement secretary categorized his life. Lynsey was older than Jenny (her veto was the final act of her office life). Lynsey was civil to Jenny when she phoned, but not warm in the way that Jenny had been towards Virginia. They did not chat. Jenny was reassured and excluded by the distance.

Emily climbed onto Richard's lap, causing him to spill his drink. Jenny used to try the same trick in the bar of the hotel they used. She would sit on Richard's lap, stroke his hair and dip her finger in his glass before poking it into his mouth. Were the waiters trained to register no surprise or curiosity, or was it instinct? Richard had small white teeth, Toby's teeth. In all other aspects, Toby took after his mother, dark eyes, classical features, lightly built.

'You're doing that thing with your mouth again,' said

Richard. His face no longer softened when he looked at her. His string lips were tight, his dimpled chin set. Emily was kicking him lazily with her right leg.

'I was just thinking,' said Jenny. 'I must get on.'

She closed the kitchen door behind her and went to her bedroom, where she found her make-up bag and applied beige foundation in little dots, generous amounts of shiny white highlighter, a favourite with Olivia Newton John, and pink 'gloss to her still heart-shaped lips. She managed to poke her mascara brush in her eye, resulting in tears which may have been there anyway.

'Let me be loved,' she whispered to her imploring face in the mirror. 'Lord, forgive me for my sins and let my husband cherish me.'

She blew out her still soft cheeks. Her make-up bag fell to the floor scattering broken crumbs of blue eye shadow onto the beige carpet. Jenny crouched down to pick them up. From this perspective she could see the reassuring pile of literature under her bed: Elegant Resorts, Classic Holidays, Ocean Tours, America with Style, Island Retreats, Luxury Landscapes. Oh, the romance of it all.

Three

Dear Madame Arnout

    As you have probably heard from Premier Villas,
I am renting your villa Compagne-sur-Mer for the last
two weeks of August. I have some information and
additional questions I would like to clarify with you.
There will be three couples – myself and my husband,
Mr and Mrs Godwin and Mr and Mrs Wharton. There
are also two teenagers, my step-son Toby and Mr and
Mrs Godwin's daughter Daisy, aged nearly eighteen.
Then there is my daughter Emily, who is nearly ten. So
we will be using all six bedrooms. Could you confirm
which is the master bedroom and whether there is a
connecting door to allow my husband and myself access
to our daughter's room? Also, Mr Wharton, is sadly
confined to a wheelchair. Could you let me know
whether there are any problems with access? I also
require information as to whether the swimming pool
gets the sun in the morning or the afternoon. One

*further thing: could you let me know what kind of linen
is available for the beds? In addition, could you inform
me whether the oven is gas or electric and about the
range of cooking utensils. This would be tremendously
helpful and is a matter of urgency.*

*We are looking forward ~~tremendously~~ very much, to
our stay; the villa looks beautiful in the brochure. Also,
could you let me know whether the pool is at the front
or back of the house and whether the drive is private or
can be accessed by anyone else? Thank you so much.
I look forward to hearing from you. As soon as possible.*

Sincerely

Jenny Wentworth (Mrs)

PS Is there a full set of kitchen knives?

The letter, was typed in double spacing on Richard's company-
headed paper to ensure respectful attention. Jenny's brow
furrowed with nurse-like sympathy at the line about the
wheelchair access. She had not realized Derek had MS when
she contacted his wife Amanda, her old school friend. It is the
sort of thing you miss if you are out of touch too long. And
since Amanda had only mentioned it after accepting the
invitation Jenny felt obliged to sound unfussed although she
fretted like mad about it, stretching her mouth like an elastic
band when she was alone. She had imagined her friends as a
loving, laughing appendage to her own marriage. They were

like dishes to present before her husband. They were there to solve problems rather than create them. She imagined that everyone else's life ticked along as hers did. She was afraid that the misfortunes of others might seep into her sandy foundations like a curse. But she was porous hearted and became quite tearful at the thought of Amanda's unluckiness. Perhaps the holiday would be a turning point for her. A rest and possibly a cure. You never knew.

> *Dear Mrs Wentworth*
>
> *Thank you for your letter. I am delighted with your visit and hope you will find everything comfortable. You will find no problems with the house arrangements. I will be here to show you around. The sun and the shade are there at your convenience. It is a very beautiful place and you will surely love the garden. Let me know of any further requirements.*
>
> *Yours*
> *Madame Arnout*
> *PS My kitchen knives are my joy and pride!*

Well there was a further requirement, as it turned out. Gerry Godwin announced that he would not after all be bringing his wife Angela but his parliamentary researcher Syrie Mussaud. He hoped Daisy would be coming pending some tricky negotiations with his wife. This was not at all what Jenny had envisaged. She had chosen her holiday companions carefully. They were to be old friends with interesting jobs, but not threateningly interesting. It was disloyal to Angela as well as destabilizing to invite one half of a marriage and his mistress. It was intolerable.

Richard took a different view.

'Well, well, who'd have thought old Gerry had it in him?' He guffawed over lamb noisettes and sliced potatoes. 'Syrie sounds a bit of a catch.'

'But we don't even know her,' said Jenny, passing him the herb salad doused in vinaigrette. 'It's the wrong mix. It won't be relaxing.'

'Sounds rather fun,' said Richard, gravy glistening on his chin. 'And I don't think we can get preachy about it. We did the same thing after all.'

Jenny felt the heat rise up her face as if she were standing over a stove. Were the origins of her marriage to be thrown back at her for ever? When would she lose the stigma and join the respectable ranks of long-term marrieds?

'It wasn't like that,' she mumbled. 'We were almost the same age, after all. Syrie is nearer in age to Daisy than she is to Gerry.'

'Ten years, twenty years, what's the difference? Gerry of all people! Crikey, good for him.' Richard laughed, shaking his head, his eyes points of light in his broad, red-beige face.

Once Richard had left Virginia, Jenny had experienced a

Pauline conversion to marriage. She regarded female threats to the institution as far more dangerous than Al Qaeda. She hated Richard's laddish sympathy for a university friend who had slipped the leash, and how much better tempered and more forgiving he was towards his friends than his family. Perhaps family brought out the worst in some people.

Dear Madame Arnout

I find it necessary to make an amendment to my initial arrangements. Mr and Mrs Godwin will require separate rooms. Is the outhouse available as a bedroom? The standard of linen there will not be so important. Is the room self-contained as appears in the floor plans?

We are all still looking forward extremely to our stay. Also to meeting you. I feel that we have a shared interest in the villa! Do let me know about the bedroom arrangements as soon as you can.

Sincerely

Jenny Wentworth

Greetings once more, Mrs Wentworth!

You are a little agitated about your party, no? I am doing business in the centre of London next week. Shall we meet for the lunch on Friday? I prefer the Chelsea restaurant called the Basket. Perhaps you could let me

know by email if this is convenient. I am very pleased
to meet you,
    Yours
    Jessica Arnout

Jenny was not at all sure that this was a good idea. She had learned the hard way what happens when you rent holiday houses from friends. Never, never again. If you mix business with pleasure you end up paying more and being friendly less. Commercial differences became misunderstandings, which are much harder to resolve. All those hurt, unfinished sentences: 'Oh, but I thought . . .' 'Well, obviously, I imagined . . .' The tight resentment in the chest.

Madame Arnout seemed to have decided Jenny was an anxious, difficult woman. This was simply not the case. One of her hallmarks as a PA had been her unflappability. Richard had said so. 'At least there is one sane person in the building,' he had once said when he had met employee resistance to his interpretation of European working legislation. Jenny had smiled sympathetically and tapped her pen against her note-book. 'No one thinks how hard it is for you to keep to the bottom line.' Richard had looked up slyly, his eyes tiny jewels encrusted in his heavy jug-like face. 'Ah yes, talking of bottom lines . . .'

Jenny could have flirted with Richard for ever. It made the working day so delightful. The thrilling awareness of another's presence. When he handed her a letter to type she thought, These manicured, business-like fingers were inside me last night, and her stomach turned to liquid. She watched Richard being masterful or vulnerable and felt she was riding his moods.

But since they married, the sexual tension of work and intimacy had evaporated. Richard was masterful or vulnerable somewhere else. By the time he got home he was simply ... spent. They did not quarrel, although their banter was border-line bickering. At dinner parties Richard had a knack of fondly undermining her. When a couple from his squash club who had young children were complaining about broken nights Richard broke in, 'Oh, Jenny always slept like a log. But now Emily is older, she's going to try to cut down her hours from sixteen to twelve!' Jenny laughed and protested, but not as keenly as she wanted to. The adjective log-like had never been applied to Olivia Newton John. The implication was that Jenny was lazy and possibly fat.

When Richard's boss, Zoe, had invited them both to supper at her vast river-side apartment in Southwark, Richard had praised the location, the decor and the food for being stylish, bold and unfussy. 'How nice to have decent grub that doesn't have five different sauces and butter shaped like a swan.' This was a travesty of Jenny's cordon bleu cooking as Richard well knew and winking, 'only joking', did not take the sting out of it. Jenny did not laugh that time, but picked her napkin up from the wooden floor to disguise acid tears. While her head was under the table she could see her husband's pinstriped thighs and noticed his flies were slightly undone. It had been one of his whispered fantasies for her to suck him off at a dinner party. Are all fantasies ironic? Why not end everything now, spectacularly, by grabbing her husband's cock under the table and noisily consuming it? She straightened up slowly and dabbed at the side of her mouth with the napkin. She was shaken by her imagined brush with domestic Armageddon. 'All right, Jen?' Richard had asked kindly.

Jenny was no longer a mistress — even of her own home. Richard had been his old persuasive, charming self when they had signed the contract for the house. There were various little clauses over which she had frowned in the solicitor's office.

'I would like you to read this carefully,' said the solicitor, who was a slight, bent man with kindly round brown eyes.

She had looked at him and then back to Richard, who was a Colossus in the small first-floor office in Wigmore Street. She put her elbows on the desk and shielded her eyes with her hands so she could concentrate. Richard was humming 'Ode to Joy' and shifting his weight so that he blocked out her light. She felt him glance at his watch.

'Ready, darling?' he said in that corporate rumble she remembered from the office. You did not keep Richard waiting. She signed her name in her steady, tidy writing and pushed the paper across the desk. She had to trust Richard.

Sometimes, when her husband was being difficult, she felt her stomach coil with anxiety at the memory of this scene. What security did she have? But on a good day, a holiday, she took a more optimistic view. Her lack of material independence bound her closer to Richard. It made divorce inconceivable.

Jenny put off her reply to Madame Arnout. She was busy with her ambitious Etruscan-style plate in pottery class. She glided round Tesco's filling her trolley to its abundant limit, loving the nurturing warmth of the pyramid of food at the till, making apologetic grimaces to the queue behind her – single people with meagre baskets of microwave meals for one.

She imagined the coarse wooden trestle table in France, the al fresco dinners that lay before her. Jenny was transported by the prospect of large bowls of salad, bread and poussins from the local market. With whom could she share her aromatic fantasies?

Why not? She crept into Richard's study and logged on to his computer.

Dear Madame Arnout
See you there. What fun!
Sincerely
Jenny Wentworth

Most of us, at some time, have made the mistake of following up a holiday friendship. Since people usually travel within their socio-economic group it is unsurprising that post codes are shared, yet the proximity is treated like destiny. 'We must meet uuuup,' couples mouth through the back windows of minibuses. 'See you back in . . .' But people usually find their lives are smaller and more settled than they imagined. There isn't room or time to cram in these new acquaintances. The mental address book is full.

To meet a holiday associate before the holiday had even begun seemed most odd to Jenny. But she parked her jeep badly in a narrow street off the Kings Road, causing apoplexy among delivery-van drivers, and hurried to the restaurant. Being lunch time mid week it was packed with women, their men folk all fighting on the front at their offices.

Jessica Arnout had not given a description of herself. She had not needed to. She would have won a spot the French-woman contest. Jessica had volcanic black hair, stretched back so fiercely that one could see the follicles pulling the pores round her hairline. She was wearing a dark grey suit with a brightly coloured scarf knotted round her neck. Despite her obvious foreign nationality, she looked familiar.

Jessica waved her cigarette at Jenny, who was flattered she had been spotted among the many lean, blonde women wearing white shirts with pastel-coloured jerseys over their shoulders. On the other hand, she was the only one carrying a brochure.

Jenny pulled back her chair and put her little chain bag and brochure under it.

'So, what business brings you to London?' she asked, a line that had come to her while she was parking.

Jessica narrowed her striking amber eyes as she inhaled on her cigarette.

'Oh, I have to visit the agency to know whether I have the satisfaction with them. And I have friends in London. Do you live near here?'

Jenny gesticulated in what she took to be a European fashion.

'Yes, I am in Chiswick, quite near Heathrow. Would you mind if I had one of your cigarettes?'

'Of course,' said Jessica handing her the packet. She produced an ugly gold lighter and flicked it in front of Jenny's face. Jenny's hand was shaking. Why? She didn't feel nervous. Now this woman would question her suitability as a tenant and the safety of her antiques. Jessica did not appear to notice, although she studied Jenny closely.

Jenny looked hard at the menu, aware of her companion's fine-skinned, thin face with its narrow, slightly hooked nose close to hers. She noticed the sharp arrow lines at the base of the Frenchwoman's forehead. This was because Jenny was considering having Botox injections and so looked for signs of it in other women in the same way as men might notice registration plates. It was a specialism. Richard's boss had definitely had Botox, Jenny had announced triumphantly on their drive home from Southwark, which somehow offset Zoe's salary and status. Perhaps it was more an American trait than a European one. Not much scope for Mediterranean expressiveness if your face was frozen. Jessica's face rippled with frowns and crow's feet as she looked quizzically across the table at Jenny Wentworth's absorbed, almost trance-like expression. Jenny's head dived like a duck's behind the menu.

The conversation was businesslike and practical. At the back of Jenny's mind was the school run and Richard's dinner. She sipped sparingly at her glass of red wine to minimize the muscle-softening effect of the alcohol.

'And the friends who are accompanying you? They are sympathetic, good companions?' asked Jessica pushing her plate of seafood to one side.

'Oh yes, good sorts, as we say here. Amanda is a very old friend of mine from school. I mean, we don't see each other so much now. We've plenty to catch up on. She has had a difficult time with her husband being so ill. I'd like to help in any way I can.'

Jenny smiled brightly and felt awful. She had not been a good friend. Did Jessica sense that? Probably not, she was too busy smoking.

'And the others?'

'Gerry is a friend of my husband. He is a government whip.'

'A whip?' asked Jessica raising an eyebrow.

'It is a parliamentary term. He keeps order. He's . . . um . . . bringing his researcher – a girl – I don't know her.'

'Ah,' said Jessica with an engaging gap-toothed smile.

'They are very respectable. She is just young, that's all.'

'Perhaps a companion for Toby and Daisy?' said Jessica.

Jenny unexpectedly bubbled with laughter.

'That's right!' she said. 'More their age. I have no idea how it will work out.'

'Men are such fools, no?' said Jessica lightly. Jenny glanced at her watch. She should be going.

'Another glass of wine?' asked Jessica.

'Oh, go on, why not?' said Jenny. She was enjoying herself. 'What about your husband? Do you have a family?' she asked.

Jessica considered the question and shook her head. 'No, it is the story of my life not to have a husband,' she said. 'Not the normal husband. But I have the nephews and I have two cats which are really, for me, like children.'

Jenny smiled serenely. What could be nicer than a sad old spinster with cats for babies? She felt the full force of the mothers' union behind her. She did not intend to convey superiority, that would be wrong, but she brimmed with graciousness.

'I am so glad to have met you,' she said. 'This holiday means so much to me, to my family. We all, our family, love that part of France. Please feel free to drop in any time. I would like you' – she dropped her eyes shyly – 'to feel part of our family.'

'Thank you,' said Jessica, pulling back her chair. 'Everyone loves their own family. It is like the expression – do you know it? – everyone likes the smell of his own fart?'

Actually Jenny did not know it and was surprised at Madame Arnout's vulgarity. Perhaps one always learned smutty phrases in a foreign language; Toby could swear in six languages. Jenny would rather have finished the conversation with a more formal pleasantry. One did not expect to issue courtly hospitality and have it thrown back in the manner of the Wife of Bath. She remembered a circular conversation with Toby when he was ten and they were watching *Grease* on video together during a custody access weekend. Toby had commented on the tightness of Olivia Newton John's black rubber suit and asked what would happen if she farted.

'It wouldn't happen, because she is Olivia Newton John,' Jenny had answered.

'But what if she did?' Toby persisted. Jenny had lost her temper, for the only time with her stepson. 'Why do you have to spoil everything?' she had shouted, putting the tape on pause.

When she turned round Toby had disappeared. Jenny had looked behind the sofa, under the table, everywhere. She had run out of the front door looking up and down the street. She finally found Toby behind the sitting-room curtains. He struggled to say through his sobs that he had caused one divorce and now he was going to bust up a second marriage. It was the chocolate buttons rather than the assurances of his blamelessness that had eventually tempted him out.

Jenny parted cordially, with kisses on both cheeks, from Jessica. She felt the encounter, slightly edited, had perked up her day and her self-esteem and could be relayed without timidity to Richard. Later, as Jenny reached the school just in time to collect Emily before the gates closed and she was officially reprimanded she realized who Jessica reminded her of: Virginia.

Four

When Jenny married Richard some of her colleagues had said, 'Oh, you'll make a wonderful wife.' Since at that time she had not embarked on her cordon bleu cookery course, and reading her email exchange with Richard gave only a snapshot of her sex life, Jenny wondered how they could know this. What were her wifely qualities? Character was a matter of reflection. If she were loved and respected she did not doubt that she would conduct herself with confidence and dignity. Without that endorsement she would feel nervous and wrongly pitched. A whole industry has been built around motivating office staff, but there is no guidance on domestic teamwork. Home is merely time out.

Jenny could only surmise that when people remarked she would be a good wife they were either being polite or were transplanting her office skills to the home. Could wifeliness be spun out of a good filing system and a pleasant telephone manner? Or did the selflessness of a first-rate PA translate into being a doormat at home? Jenny felt she had never found an appropriate personality for home. It was not her domain, although it was the territory she had wanted to conquer more than anywhere in the world.

Still, Jenny's gift for packaging which had served her so well in the past had not deserted her. She had used more tissue paper than the General Trading Company during her move to Chiswick. Her other contribution was labelling, which she did with rainbow-coloured marker pens. The unpacking of Richard's boxes was more complicated and melancholy. She had hoped he would leave all his things with Virginia, allowing them a fresh start. But the past filtered through with books inscribed to 'R from V', paintings dated on the back (wedding anniversaries) and innocent-looking pieces of silver which turned out to be Toby's christening presents. Oh, and eight years' worth of holiday photographs: Toby in water wings, Virginia holding up a towel for him, Virginia with her head on Richard's shoulder, laughing at a forgotten joke told outside an unspecified European cafe.

The lightest box was marked 'Toby's Overnight Things'. This contained two pairs of blue football-motif pyjamas, a toy lion, an Arsenal dressing grown with the belt missing, a yellow plastic torch, one Arsenal poster and two Jennings' paperbacks.

Jenny's holiday methodology involved intensive periods of research (within narrow criteria), followed by the actual booking, followed by a period of semi-consciousness when she floated through the early summer months in the knowledge that something lovely was going to happen. She knew the best holidays had an element of effort and reward (actually the best holidays were contained in the back of the luxury supplements of glossy magazines, but that was a future aspiration). So, at the beginning of July, Jenny started her 'regime'. Her meals began to contain a great deal of celery and cucumber, and she began her offices exercises as recommended by the *Daily Mail*. As a secretary, she had been familiar with rotating her ankles under her desk and lifting files with a flat, outstretched arm. Jenny had perfected a household version of these stretches and weights, using rolling pins and books. She bent and stretched her knees while cooking and lifted her leg behind her as she wiped the kitchen surfaces. She was surprised to see Emily clasping her hands over her head and squatting in front of the television. The *Daily Mail* had emphasized that these exercises were invisible to others.

Jenny also cut down on her shopping bill, using cheaper cuts of meat or coarser olive oil so that she could justify the buying of sarongs, sun creams and baseball hats.

Moreover, she had finally decided to opt for Botox. Wasn't it just a very expensive form of acupuncture? She made an appointment at the smartest of Chiswick's beauty salons and then phoned back twice to change her mind and once to change her name to Jenny Newton, just in case one of the school-run mothers noticed her in the appointment book.

Jenny took her place in the waiting room with a copy of *Traveller* magazine held high in front of her face. Thank heavens, no one she knew was there. She hoped no paparazzi were waiting outside in an attempt to catch an actress coming out so they could publish the photograph with the headline: 'Do you still deny having cosmetic surgery?' Jenny loved the *Daily Mail*'s pursuit of wealthy or professional women, but she didn't want to get caught up in friendly fire as she hurried from the salon to her car.

When she came out, she got in the jeep and locked the doors, glanced around and then examined herself in the mirror. Her skin looked slightly reddened. She frowned and smiled; nothing had changed. Three days later her face began to set like cooked cake mixture. When Emily poked her in the eye by mistake with a paintbrush and when Richard forgot their anniversary dinner, Jenny displayed an impressive outward stoicism. In fact, she was expressionless.

August 14 was a day of absolute contentment. It was time to pack.

Jenny's Suitcase
1 black swimming costume

The Villa

1 flowery swimming costume
1 high-leg bikini for possible use in second week
Underwear
1 new sarong
1 last year sarong
5 T-shirts (3 new)
2 daytime sun dresses
1 full-length black jersey dress (new)
3 pairs shoes (2 casual)
3 pairs shorts (1 new)
2 pairs capri pants
2 sweaters
1 suede jacket (the unsuitable item)
Accessories
Hat!
Books (Domestic Bliss or the Bitch in the House – *and a*
Booker prize-winner, name forgotten)

She closed her neat suitcase with pride.

Then she unpacked underwear and two shirts from Richard's suitcase that he had left there after a previous trip, and checked all screwed-up receipts and plane tickets for obvious reasons.

Richard's Suitcase
2 pairs swimming trunks

10 T-shirts
5 shirts
5 pairs shorts
3 pairs trousers
Underwear
Socks
3 pairs shoes
1 linen suit
2 sweaters
After-sun care
Phone charger
Wires and cable from the bedroom floor, possibly for laptop
Hat!
The Day of the Jackal
Condoms?

Emily's Suitcase
3 swimming costumes
1 pair frog goggles
10 plain T-shirts
5 with slogans
5 pairs shorts
5 pairs cotton trousers
4 sweaters
3 pairs pyjamas
5 pairs flowery pants

5 pairs television-character pants
Matching socks
Jelly shoes
Sandals
Soft toys (must ask which is current favourite)
Hat!
Carole Vorderman maths books
Illustrated French dictionary
Recommended reading list – 6 books

There were sand and shells at the bottom of Emily's suit-case: memories of far-away countries. Jenny's heart was adrift with serenity.

She had one final appointment, a holiday aperitif: a facial. Jenny often said to herself that if she suffered a ghastly economic misfortune and was forced to cancel one or more of her annual holidays, then she would make it up to herself with a facial. It was an indulgence that eclipsed food or sex. She wondered if it came close to a lesbian experience. Comfort, kindness and gentle non-invasive hands. She trotted into the heated dimly lit room and climbed onto the treatment bed. It was like a maternity hospital but without the pain, noise and demands. Here the white-coated women were like fantasy nurses. A tape clicked on with some kind of singing whale music. She felt long cool hands cup her face and a slather of cream form loose circles on her cheeks. She drifted in and out of consciousness, her eyelids flickering as thoughts rose from the deep – cancel milk – Syrie a pain in the arse – have I locked the car? – will this dislodge the Botox so it floats around my face freezing an eye or a cheek at random and making me look neuralgic? These were not perhaps the same meditative patterns as those of Buddhist monks, but it was the nearest she got to a religious experience. Upward strokes on her neck, pressure on her temples, tissues floating over her face mopping up excess moisture. The rough caress of warm, white towels. Then it was over. Jenny stretched and scratched her head. 'Mmm, that was *so* relaxing. It was so good.'

'Have you got much on today?' asked the quiet, self-possessed beautician as she went to wash her hands at the sink. Oh, the level of cleanliness in these places! It was better than a hospital; it was like a laboratory.

'Yes,' sighed Jenny. 'I am very busy.'

The beautician nodded sympathetically. She was not censorious about Jenny's life. Walking down the street was considered stressful by these angels of mercy. The world was big and dirty and full of men. The facial clinic was a modern convent.

*

This was a good day. A day of feeling calm and pure, relaxed, energetic and centred. Jenny saw beauty treatments as a means to an end rather than a way of life. She wanted to shine from within, not because she owed it to herself, but because Toby was coming round for dinner

She cooked chicken and rice because Toby had always liked chicken as a child. Initially, Jenny had treated him a little like Hansel, luring him into her home with promises of edibility. She had made cakes in the shapes of cartoon characters and rocket-shaped biscuits (later, booby-shaped biscuits for a real laugh). She had introduced him to curries and flipped pancakes for him. Cooking for her was a form of flirtation. She knew Virginia cooked to nourish rather than to titillate. The way to a man's heart is through his imagination.

So tonight it was spicy chicken and a heavy chocolate desert from Nigella Lawson. She hadn't decided whether to attribute this dish. Obviously she would like the phrase Domestic Goddess bandied round the dinner table; on the other hand there were no physical similarities between her and Nigella. You had to pick a style, and Jenny had spent many years being Olivia Newton John. There was too much difference between Olivia and Nigella Lawson. She therefore rather resented Nigella and would say defiantly, 'I really don't think she is attractive,' as she put her books back on the shelf. Jenny had found she could guide men, or at least Richard, in their opinion on these things. She acted as a filter, a search engine. Richard could only find other women attractive through her.

The doorbell rang and Emily's footsteps pummelled the floor as she ran to answer it. Jenny smiled as she heard Toby's youthful deep voice. Not so long since that voice had broken. She remembered the transparent anxiety with which he asked of other boys mentioned in conversation, 'Has his voice broken?' Jenny might have missed out on the beginning of Toby's life but, like piano grades, all the interesting material came later on. Why had she thought of the piano? Damn Virginia. She wiped her hands on a tea towel and waited for Emily to pull Toby into the kitchen.

'Hey!' he said, as he dipped his head instinctively in the doorway.

His teeth shone under the ceiling lights. Jenny remembered exactly when, more or less, they had been released from braces. She had taken a close interest in his orthodontic development. She liked to claim credit for his teeth.

'It may be expensive, but teeth are for ever!' she would say to Richard as she inspected her own in the bathroom mirror. She said this, knowing that Richard had at least two that were capped. She loved Richard, but like all spouses, she constantly drew implicit, often vicarious attention to her virtues and the other's weaknesses.

'If you can give them a good education and good teeth they are set up for life!' This was a borrowed truth she had heard from an expensive-looking blonde woman at the gym. Jenny had been at the next table in the bar area, flicking through a magazine and drinking energy juice. She had looked up and smiled with appreciative sympathy but the blonde had blanked her. Did the blonde look more like Olivia Newton John than she? On balance, Jenny didn't think so.

'Hi, Toby! You look so well! What have you done to your hair? It's like, it's like Prince Harry. No, who do I mean? Busted or someone?'

'Mum,' said Emily gravely, 'you are so embarrassing. Toby's hair is just normal. It's not a style.'

'It's OK.' Toby smiled, indulgently polite towards the social fumbling of adults.

'Well, what's your news?' asked Jenny cocking her head and immediately realizing that this was a conversation stopper. She had to relax, to accept that the balance of power between generations had shifted. It was Toby who needed to lead the way. In fact, let's face it, he had been the stronger partner for years.

'Not much news really, pretty quiet. Mum's done a lot of planting, you know, so hope the weather holds. I've had exams.'

'Of course!' mouthed Jenny. Why hadn't she thought of that? The young were always having exams. They were ongoing. She could never remember their names. She had given up ever trying to remember which form Toby and then Emily were in. (She had once asked Richard which class Emily was in for a school trip and he replied, 'Oh, I should say middle. Put upper middle.' It must have been a time when he thought Jenny worth expending jokes on.) The changing combination of figures and letters defeated her. In the same way, she was hazy about her daughter's inoculation dates. Data was so easy to assemble in the office and so hard to keep track of at home. Jenny frowned. She needed a better filing system for her thoughts. They were all over the place, in any old chronological order.

Emily had once told her mother that her best friend at school was Maxine Carr and her favourite subject was MTV studies. As a result, Jenny had said to Emily's form teacher at a parents' evening that she was pleased Emily had found such a loyal friend but she hadn't seen any of her MTV homework. Ha ha funny not ha ha peculiar. How Richard and Emily had laughed. But was it a terrible thing to believe what people told you?

Toby agreed. 'Jenny's a sort of innocent,' he had said shrugging his shoulders.

'Sit down, have a glass of beer. Emily, do let Toby eat.'

Five

The country had gone holiday mad. The newspapers were full of stories about threatened strikes by air traffic controllers and pictures of celebrities in their bikinis. The school term had ended and parliament had risen for the summer. The most widely read news page was the world weather forecasts. Jenny was proud she could finally understand centigrade. It was a secret alliance she had forged with the children against Richard.

'Wow, it is twenty-nine in Avignon already,' she said, first thing one morning.

Richard grunted as he searched under the bed for his phone charger. Where the hell was it? By advertising his accessibility he hoped to disguise the fact that he was on holiday. His other trick was to send emails to colleagues containing his dates of absence that missed out weekends. 'I shall be out of the office from 1 to 5 August inclusive and from 7 to 11.' The purpose was to confuse family holidays with client golf trips – a necessary corporate cover. He became increasingly irritable as the day of departure approached and no work crisis could be conjured to excuse him from going. He was happiest following the family out a couple of days later and returning home early – alone and in business class. Richard loved his family very much, but preferred them diluted with work. He was a little afraid of long periods alone with Jenny. It was like being stuck in a cage with a canary. She was very pretty, but nervous and needy – and a bit silly. He did not regret marrying her, of course not, it had been his decision and he stood by it. Plus, Jenny had given him an enchanting daughter. But occasionally he dreamt he was still married to Virginia and when he awoke he felt oddly choked.

Richard told himself he probably needed a break. When he asked Jenny if she had packed his book, she knew he had surrendered.

Jenny had chuckled with Virginia over Richard's collapsing resistance to a holiday when she had dropped off some T-shirts for Toby the evening before. Jenny liked a reason to see Virginia, partly because she yearned for a friendship which could never be realized and partly because she enjoyed a quick snoop round her house. She could not help making comparisons. Virginia's house – the family home – in Wandsworth was, on the face of it, more valuable, but Jenny reckoned her new conservatory had evened things up. That and the subtle disrepair which inevitably occurred when the main breadwinner left home. Virginia's rust-pink front door was peeling and the kitchen cupboard doors sloped from their hinges. She did not seem to mind. Her fingers were grimy with soil from her garden and her hair was grey at the edge (a luxury of first wives). She hummed a piece of Chopin she had been playing on the piano.

'So you're all packed?' she asked in her too low to be properly feminine voice.

'We are.' Jenny grimaced. 'I just hope it isn't going to be too hot.'

She felt obliged to say something negative about the holiday in case Virginia was envious, although she displayed no signs of it. But you couldn't tell. The civility between the two women prevented depths of warmth or animosity. The relationship between first and second wives should not be prodded. Jenny felt free to enter Virginia's house, but knew she was expected to refuse the offer of a drink. She could collect or drop off things or children, but go no further. This was the unwritten rule.

At first, she had thought a new partner for Virginia would shift the balance. She told Richard she hoped Virginia would find someone else, subtly implying that it was a tall order. Virginia's refusal to do so had become a reproach of a different kind. She seemed genuinely self-sufficient. It was Jenny who had failed to find a new equilibrium.

When she drove off, she looked back in the mirror at the tall, thoughtful figure resting against the door and felt dissatisfied. Perhaps she had done Virginia a favour. Then she slapped her wrist, which was greasy and noxious smelling from the fake-tan spray she had applied. What a mean-spirited woman she was. What an irritating, silly woman. She slowed down and momentarily considered reversing up the road and begging Virginia for forgiveness. But Virginia had gone back inside. Jenny breathed through one nostril and then the other. Be calm, be centred, think of the waves lapping quietly on the peroxide sand.

'I am a nice person,' she whimpered.

The Eurostar train left at 7.30 a.m. At five, Jenny rose quietly and made her final pre-holiday preparations. It felt like a wedding day without the intimidation of guests. There was something preordained about the morning: she checked the tickets and passports in her nylon folder; she went and made a cup of tea, singing to herself.

'You're the one that I want, honey, ooh, ooh, ooh.'

Milkman cancelled, newsagent alerted, menstrual cycle diverted. Thank goodness she did not have pets to worry about any more. There had been experiments – hamsters, puppies – symbols of a warm family life. All had been returned after explosions of irritation from Richard and a stoical shrug from Emily. Quite a relief, actually.

Jenny opened the conservatory doors, which were a little stiff and looked out at the bright morning. She wondered if Amanda was up yet. Did she have to wash and dress her husband? Was it awkward getting a wheelchair into a taxi? Jenny had vowed to take a Red Cross first-aid course but had never got around to it. She was a little alarmed by the disabled. Obviously she intervened if a person with a white stick was tapping too close to a parked car – for the sake of the blind person and of the car. She thought her tone of voice was quite good. But she would not actually cross the road to help. She pretended she had not seen them and then felt awful afterwards. She hoped she would get it right on holiday and not fuss too much. There was an art to dealing with the disabled, to offering practical assistance without betraying pity. It made her nervous.

She thought of Gerry waking to the sound of an alarm clock. Did he crack on, or roll over for some fetid, intergenerational sex? She shuddered. Oh, it was going to be a challenge this holiday, it was not well cast.

She thought of Toby, who was arriving with Daisy on a cheap flight, luridly advertised. It had been Toby's suggestion, so Daisy wouldn't have to miss her best friend's nineteenth birthday party the night before. Thus, he had quietly defused the first holiday time bomb of Daisy having to travel with Syrie and her father, a prospect which had provoked tears from Daisy and a Joan of Arc display of martyrdom from her mother.

Jenny's shoulders relaxed and she smiled at the thought of Toby. When she had told her yoga class about the villa they had singled out the teenagers as the potential source of tension. Jenny had tried to explain that adults were the adolescents so far as she was concerned – less attractive and harder to talk to. Her class had suspected her of being witty.

Footsteps pattered down the stairs and the door handle to the kitchen turned. Emily yawned and stretched as she found her bearings. Her hair was matted and slightly electrocuted-looking. It was not simply parental tyranny that forced children to brush their hair. Somehow their hair needed brushing more than adults'. Why was that?

'Are we going on holiday today?' Emily sighed, widening her eyes and poking her finger into her nose. It was solely parental tyranny that prevented children from behaving like chimpanzees.

'Yes, darling, I've put your clothes out for you on the chair.'

'I'm wearing this,' she said, sleepily determined. Jenny sighed.

By 6.30 a.m. the group were on the platform at Waterloo. Amanda and Derek were travelling by air. Jenny was wearing flowery pedal pushers, a crisp white shirt and sandals. She had a metallic-coloured varnish on her toenails. She had switched manicure salons some months ago after the owner of her local was shot by her lover's wife. It had made the papers and brightened up the school run. Jenny was carrying her sun visor, which she planned to pop on once they were out of the Channel Tunnel. Richard stood guard over his golf clubs, wearing the baggy shorts and polo shirt Jenny had assigned to him. Emily sat on the cases in her Buffy the Vampire pyjamas and trainers, her head bent over *Harry Potter*. Who could doubt their family credentials? Jenny gave Richard a flirtatious shove.

'Look at me, I'm Sandra Dee,' she sang playfully, mimicking the scene from *Grease*. He patted her bottom. Jenny felt as if she was in a brightly coloured air balloon looking down at her far-away day to day existence. She was on holiday. She was carefree.

'Due to persons on the line at Dover this train is delayed until further notice. We apologize for the delay. This is due to . . .' the voice crackled and disappeared. It returned with sudden clarity, 'We apologize to passengers waiting to board the Eurostar train. There are persons on the line at Dover. Please wait for a further announcement. Tea and coffee are available at the buffet.'

'Oh, for Christ's sake,' said Richard, glaring at the train, and whipping out his mobile from his pocket.

Emily looked up from her book.

'Maybe it's Voldemort,' she said, widening her eyes.

'Bloody asylum seekers,' grunted Richard, holding his phone like a paperweight in his palm. He turned to office toys in times of stress.

'It is so selfish,' agreed Jenny vehemently.

'Mummy, I'm sure the persons don't want to be on the railway line,' whispered Emily reproachfully. 'I'm sure they would rather travel on the train. But they don't have the money.'

'Emily you don't understand. You can't just turn up in somebody else's country.'

'But we are. In France,' argued Emily.

'Oh, don't be so silly. We're going on holiday. We're bringing money into France.'

'But what if you don't have any money?'

'Then you don't go on holiday. I mean migrate. You save up. Or something. It is too complicated to explain Emily. I am not in the mood for this.'

'Why didn't we fly?' asked Richard disinterestedly.

Jenny eyed her husband suspiciously. Was he blaming her because a bunch of Kurds had decided to walk through the Channel Tunnel? She slipped into her soothing sing-song secretarial voice, 'Do you remember, I looked into flights, but there was the air traffic controllers' threat. There may not even be any flights.'

'So are we not going on holiday then?' asked Emily.

'Of course we are,' her parents chorused. 'Don't be silly.'

'I'm going to go and find out what the hell is going on,' said Richard walking purposefully towards the ticket office. The illusion of purpose was his defence mechanism.

The platform was now heaving with holiday makers sighing and tapping their feet as if collective irritation could shift the placidly unmoving train.

Jenny's head was beginning to ache. Could the desperation of the few justify the inconvenience of the many? She would have liked to feel empathy, for she was not a heartless woman. But if the Kurds (which is what she had decided they were) cared nothing for her, why should she care about them? Holidays were an insulation against the world. There was only so much quality of life to go round, and she was not prepared to give hers away.

Richard was pushing through the crowd towards her. His face was ruddy and a pendulum of sweat shone on his cheek.

'Get the luggage into the far carriage,' he barked. 'We're about to leave.'

*

Not so bad after all. Jenny gazed out of the window at the spacious rural landscape. Farrow & Ball colours she thought to herself.

'It's like a Van Gogh painting isn't it?' she said out loud.

Richard was studying his book, his eyebrows raised in surprise over *The Day of the Jackal* whose plot he knew by heart. His chin sunk thickly into his neck. He was an imposing man with no fearful flabbiness, just a bit of subsidence. Emily read quite differently, her sapling fingers curled over the book, her eyes flicking sternly across the pages.

Jenny sighed and adjusted the home-decoration magazine on her lap. She did not feel much like reading; her mind skated over things. She gave Emily the squiffy smile she reserved for her when her daughter was being no trouble. She felt smiley and sleepy, with only a niggling of discontent that it wasn't perfect yet. The sun beat through the glass and she turned her face upwards. She put her sun visor on, then took it off again. Almost happy. Not quite. Not yet. Happiness was always in the anticipation and in the hindsight, rarely in the moment. Jenny increasingly sought adventure accompanied by total comfort and security and saw no paradox in this.

When Jenny awoke, the train was half an hour from their destination. The featureless landscape of central France had now become picturesque. Craggy mountain ranges, forests, hilltop villages, romantic towers rising above pink tiled roofs of houses like a child's drawing. She started bustling about with bags and water bottles and liberal application of hand cream. She took out her brochure and fretted about possible discrepancies. Then they were in a taxi bumping along stony tracks, past cypresses and scorched fields beyond. The house was visible on a hill above them. Emily moved onto her lap, a suction pad of sweat. The house was both true to the picture and distorted. There were the lavender pots, although the courtyard was smaller than Jenny had imagined and the thick stone villa more squat. The shutters were more lilac than blue. 'A haven of tranquillity.' The phrase hovered in Jenny's mind.

'The key isn't here. It's meant to be under the stone,' she said.

'The door is open,' said Richard.

They entered the cool, dark, central hallway. There were two suitcases by the oak chair and voices from the terrace at the back of the house. Jenny stiffened and put on her animated, hostess smile. A tall, slim figure looked at her through the open doors and mimed a greeting. It was a woman with short dark hair and sunglasses pushed up on her head. She was slightly too haggard to be pretty. Attractive then.

'Amanda!' cried Jenny grasping the woman's thin shoulders and kissing her smooth, indented cheeks. She breathed in the unfamiliar perfume. 'You haven't changed a bit!' Amanda's deep-set hazel eyes were certainly distinct, although the pathways surrounding them were new as were the deep lines from her nose to her mouth. That was the trouble with misfortune, thought Jenny. It was so ageing.

She looked past her friend to the man in the wheelchair. He looked even older, his combed hair very thin and sludge grey, his face sunken, his eyes intelligent behind thick glasses. He was wearing an open-necked pink shirt and wool trousers. Jenny glanced at the thin legs and quickly back to his face.

'You look well, Derek!' she exclaimed and grasped his clammy hand.

'Do I?' he replied, pleased.

'Richard?' announced Amanda brightly.

The reassuringly bulky shape of Jenny's husband moved forward.

'Derek, good chap. Amanda. Let me fix you a drink.'

'In the carrier bag,' fluttered Jenny. 'Let's find some ice. Well, here we all are. Isn't this nice?'

The house was assuming an independent existence from the brochure. The stone terrace had a vertiginous view of low hazy purple hills and beyond them the sky or the sea. Large iron pots contained sunflowers and figs. Jenny murmured by rote, 'A magnificent spot in which to unwind with a glass of chilled rosé . . .' There were glasses on the trestle table, Emily's book had been thrown down on the square lawn at the side of the house, leading to the (slightly smaller than described) pool. A blue-grey light settled on the landscape and a warm breeze rustled through the olive trees. Jenny felt both weary and rested, a combination of the journey and the new climate. She ostentatiously allowed Richard to carry out drinks and bread and cheese from the fridge, a sign she thought of a relaxed and successful marriage.

'Oh, the journey!' she clucked. 'An hour and half's delay. Asylum seekers at Dover! What a nightmare!'

Amanda shook her head. 'Our flight was very smooth,' she said.

Jenny flinched: partly because it was becomingly cheerful of her friend to make light of the paraphernalia of invalid travelling, and partly because it was a better gamble to fly. Jenny was meant to be the holiday connoisseur. Surely she did not wish her poor friend to have had the harder journey? She stretched her mouth wide in remorse. This was the trouble with mixing with the less fortunate: the hypersensitivity and the guilt. She was sorry, sorry, sorry.

'So it is banking you're in,' she said, pushing the olives and bread across the table at her friend.

'Financial services.' Amanda nodded. 'I run a personal consultancy.'

'No point in explaining to Jenny,' boomed Richard, tipping back his chair. 'She only knows about the City or interior decorating, isn't that right, my love?'

Jenny gave a dignified shrug. It would take a bit of time to adapt to her husband in holiday mood. What seemed authoritative in a suit, could be boorish in shorts and a sports shirt. The heat rash spreading across Richard's neck accentuated his Englishness. The environment did not suit him. She shook herself. She had forgotten to view him through loyal, conjugal eyes. Only a disinterested stranger would describe him as a heavy, hearty, nettled Englishman; Jenny knew better. He was her beloved husband and he was teasing her.

'I'm keen on pottery,' she said to Amanda. 'That's what he means.'

She turned her head the other way to include Derek in the remark. She must remember to address him directly rather than treating Amanda as his translator. It was just that his speech was slightly slurred and sometimes hard to decipher.

A car skidded on the gravel drive, doors slammed and steps echoed on the stone. Richard grinned.

'You can hear the Grand Prix from here. That'll be Gerry.'

A tall, thin man with receding hair, wearing a patterned short-sleeved shirt flapping over chinos and sandals, wandered onto the terrace. Behind him was a petite black-haired woman in a pale pink, linen sundress.

'Gerry,' said Jenny, in a tone combining reserve and familiarity.

'Helloo, Jenny. Hellooo, you must be Amanda. Meet Syrie,

here she is, come and say helloo, darling. You'll meet Daisy later, she and Toby are coming on a cattle truck.'

Amanda stood up primly.

'Nice to meet you. This is my husband Derek.'

Gerry nodded but kept his eyes fixed on the neat figure next to him. Syrie's arms were folded sceptically, her smooth face expressionless. Only her mouth moved. For heaven's sake, thought Jenny. She's chewing gum.

'Great place. Where did you find it, Jenny?' said Gerry.

'Hey, hey, hey, my old mucker, look at you, still built like a shithouse.'

Gerry and Richard slapped each other on the back.

'Syrie, this is Richard, one of my oldest friends.'

'For my sins,' said Richard, lifting Syrie's slender brown arm and kissing her hand. Jenny looked at Amanda, who was smiling sadly.

'Well, now we've all met, let's do some serious drinking. What'll you have Gerry, whisky or this European federalist stuff?'

'No good this half in half out of Europe, you reactionary old bastard,' said Gerry. 'Let's toast the European Union with some good French plonk.'

'We haven't all met,' said Amanda pleasantly. 'I haven't seen Emily yet.'

'Of course!' said Jenny. 'Emily. I'll give her a shout, there must be something here she can eat. Emileeeeee! Emileeee.' She shaded her eyes with her hand. 'I'll go and fetch her.'

She picked up her glass of wine and walked barefoot to the pool. Usually Emily would have jumped straight in, she must have found something to distract her. The grounds of the villa were quite small so, having tiptoed round the perimeter of the pool and dipped her foot in and listened contentedly to the plop of a ripple, she had to walk back past her guests.

'Shall I come with you?' asked Amanda calmly.

Jenny did not really want Amanda to tour the house with her in case aggrieved comparisons were made between the bedrooms.

'Don't worry, I'll fish her out,' she said.

Syrie was gesticulating at Richard in passionate defence of the European Union. He grinned back at her sheepishly.

'Richard, can you just check Emily hasn't wandered down the drive?' said Jenny with glassy brightness. He heaved himself reluctantly from the chair and wandered off round the side of the house, scratching his hair.

So these were the facts of the house: the hallway, cool, pleasant, pale, minimalist; the galley kitchen pristine although short of surface space. Jenny and Richard's bedroom up a flight of stone steps. Terrace view! Airy bathroom with heavy roll-topped bath. Lilac towels. Connecting bedroom, with small maple-wood bed and heavy oak chest. 'Emily? Emileee.'

Amanda and Derek's room. Smaller, darker, facing the

courtyard. Justifiable on grounds of disabled access. Large bathroom, possibly nicer than Jenny's. 'Emileeee.'

Opposite Gerry – and Syrie. Large shutters. Soundproof?

Two smaller single rooms, plain, cool, with blue shutters. No room for Emily to hide here. Jenny investigated further. A small door opened into an outhouse. Rough whitewashed walls, an old oven, pieces of stored furniture, an unmade bed. Through an alcove was a sofa piled with sheets and towels. Jenny grinned.

'Emily, come on, darling, where are you?'

The room was silent. Jenny turned and made her way back to the hallway. Richard was standing with his hands on his hips.

'Found her?' he asked.

Jenny shook her head.

'She must have wandered off.'

'She's been gone about an hour,' said Richard, his eyes cobalt blue and accusing.

Was Jenny to blame? Who was responsible when both parents were present? Jenny.

'Well, there is no need to panic. She's a sensible girl. She'll be here somewhere.'

Richard turned and walked quickly back to the terrace. He took his mobile from his pocket as he did so, like a comfort blanket.

Jenny walked out of the front. It was embracingly warm

and pretty, but she was itchy with anxiety and irritation. Emily would turn up, but until she did Jenny's chest was constricted. She lifted her sunglasses and surveyed the empty drive and miles and miles of bloody scenery.

Where, where, where? She set off barefoot, the little stones and pine needles jabbed at her heels. Her eyes stung with sun cream and the beginnings of tears. It was quiet except for the chirping of cicadas like demented chicks. She stumbled on, her mind a picture gallery of possibilities: Emily's junior-sized coffin being carried up the aisle; Jenny's defence, permissible in a coroner's court, unforgivable in the court of motherhood. She pictured Emily's open suitcase of clean clothes, identifying her at the school gates from the crowd of faces, Emily solemnly laying out her toys on her bedroom carpet, Emily being born.

Jenny's breaths grew hoarser. Where, where, where? Emily floating in a river. But there were no rivers and Emily could swim. Emily bleeding unstoppably in an animal trap. There were no farms in the vicinity. Emily trustingly putting her hand into a man's hand; a man with a van parked nearby. Jenny gasped.

'Please, please, God, let me find Emily.'

She made some deals: if Emily came back she would willingly get cancer or give more to charity, whichever God thought more useful to him.

Jenny was both nauseous with imagination and rationally

confident of Emily's well being. She was too superstitious not to confront the possibility of death, although she knew her daughter was alive. But where, where, where?

She stumbled back to the house. There were voices, but none of them high and sweet. Richard and Gerry were standing like guards in front of a slight, dark-skinned man.

'Who is this?' asked Jenny, her voice translated by fear into a screech.

'My name is Ahmed,' said the man glancing at her with large, melancholy eyes. His arms, flecked with blue and red paint, were behind his back as if tied, his head bowed. Jenny noticed that he was good-looking and chided herself for such an irrelevant observation.

'Ahmed was down by the pool house,' said Gerry.

'We are simply trying to establish what exactly he was doing there.'

'What the fuck have you done with our daughter?' said Richard, his face centimetres away from the Ahmed's carved features.

'You don't think . . .' whispered Jenny.

'I just wanna know, Ahmed. I just wanna know. Because I reckon you've seen Emily. You had to. Just tell me.'

Richard's voice broke. Jenny started to shake. Did newspaper stories happen? Did abductions, murders, happen to real children, her children?

'Perhaps we should phone the police,' said Gerry, commandingly, as if in a large office overlooking Westminster. Jenny blinked at him.

Richard stood back and examined his cell phone. Jenny's wavery mind registered that he would not be able to work out the codes. She could not remember whether he could even speak French. Virginia would have known. She could not think.

'Give me the phone,' she said and Richard wordlessly handed it to her. She looked at the swanky silver object through a mist; she was blind with fear.

'I no see Emily.' The man shrugged wearily.

'I don't believe you,' said Richard harshly.

Amanda put her hand on Richard's shoulder.

'Shouldn't we keep looking? Ahmed could stay here, but we should carry on looking. It may be that—'

'She's right,' offered Derek.

Richard shook her off.

'Phone the police, Jenny.'

A door slammed behind them. The group turned in slow motion. Footsteps, some long, some short, tapped across the stone.

'Hi, everybody,' said Toby. 'We made it.'

'Thanks to me,' said Emily, jumping onto Toby's back. 'They kept driving past the entrance, but I saw them and ran after them. What's my present, Toby? I got you here.'

'Are you all all right?' said Toby, smiling at the tense group. 'OK, Em, up, up, you go, onto my shoulders. I'm going to throw you into the pool.'

'Hi, Dad, how was your journey?' said a fresh-faced teenage girl with a bush of fair, curly hair, a shrunken T-shirt that read 'Girlpower' and low-waisted trousers, which dragged on the ground.

'Daisy,' said Gerry. 'Daisy, say hi to Syrie.'

Daisy offered her hand in acknowledgement, obviously embarrassed by the situation.

'Toby,' said Richard. 'Thank God.'

'Ahmed,' said Jenny. 'We are so very sorry for detaining you. I am sure you have work to do.'

Ahmed gave her a heavy lidded stare. He rolled his mouth at her. Oh, thought Jenny, he's going to spit at me. He pushed up his top lip showing starch-white teeth. Then he waved an arm dismissively at the company and took off. The group watched him disappear through a gate and over the hill.

'He's cute,' said Syrie, cracking gum in the side of her small mouth. 'What is he, Algerian? Just as well he doesn't have access to a lawyer.'

'Could have been nasty,' said Gerry. 'Wouldn't have looked good. The lesson is not to panic.'

There was a heavy splash from the pool, followed by squeals. Emily flung her arms round Toby's neck as he sank beneath the water.

'Oh, oh, I'll get you I'll get you,' she gasped, thrashing like a cat. 'I want to stand on your head. Toby, stay down! I am— Toby! Ooaaah!'

Jenny blew out her cheeks. That was the thing about children. They raced up and down the Richter scale: they broke your heart one moment and bored you the next.

Absolutely calm, she went to fetch candles for the table and some more glasses. She hoped God had forgotten the sacrifices offered to him in the melting point of the moment. Jenny looked in the cupboard full of rough hand-painted breakfast plates. The design was primitive and lovely. Blue, with bold red and brown figs painted round the edge. Then she went to her bedroom to spray her ankles with insect repellent. The dusk, the cloying, unpleasant smell of the spray and the laughter outside infused her. Was this happiness or relief?

As she trotted out to the terrace with more bread, and a plate of tomatoes soaked in oil and basil, poor but not very helpful Amanda was talking animatedly in the half light to Toby (probably trying to sell him life insurance); Richard was holding forth about what the government should do, while Gerry was shouting over him; Syrie was humming the 'Marseillaise' (irritatingly); Daisy was contentedly picking at her belly button and Emily was stretched out asleep on the grass. Jenny sat down gingerly next to Derek.

'It is nice to meet you properly,' she said.

The candles lit the centre of his face, which was oddly varnished and unscathed by the assault of disease on his body.

'Amanda has often spoken about you.' He smiled. 'But I thought you might be wearing a gym slip and have plaits.'

Jenny threw back her head and laughed, signalling her presence to the rest of the group.

'It has been an awfully long time. We've all been so busy. That's why I thought this holiday might be a good idea. To relax and catch up.'

Her eyes darted round the table. It was too late in the evening to start relaxing. She had better start the next day.

'I should take Emily to bed,' she said, clicking her tongue as if chivvying up a pony. She got up and bent over Emily's still form. She would be eaten alive by mosquitoes.

'Come on, darling,' she murmured, shoving one hand under Emily's knees and the other beneath her shoulder blades. She lifted her unsteadily and carried her like a lifeguard towards the house.

'Shall I take her?' offered Toby.

Jenny would not give the child up. Emily grunted a sleep-filled protest, half opened her eyes and sank back against her mother.

Jenny carried her to the bed and slipped her beneath the sheets, filthy feet first. She looked down at her transparent complexion and determined features.

'Our Father,' she whispered. 'Who art in heaven . . .'

She sighed and looked round the unfamiliar room. This was to be their home.

'Hallowed be thy name. Forgive us our trespasses.' No, she had missed a bit. 'Our Father. Thy Kingdom come.'

More laughter outside, more shouting; Jenny would not go back out there. She had missed out on the evening bonding session. Someone had to do the work.

'For thine is the Kingdom.' Oh, where was she? Jenny yawned. She must get to the market tomorrow. So much to do. She wanted Richard to come to bed. What would become of their marriage? What would become of her? She must ask Madame Arnout about Ahmed. Jenny would make it up to him. 'Forgive us our trespasses. Amen.'

Jenny unpacked enough skin creams to fill a chemist's shop and arranged them on the stone shelf in the bathroom. She ducked under the shutters and tried to close them from below. The voices were quite close. She heard her name mentioned and crouched still.

'Jenny chose the place. I leave everything to her, just hand over the cheques,' Richard said, his voice several decibels louder than when sober.

'Hey, why don't you get off your arse and help?' said Syrie. 'I wouldn't let a man get away with it.'

'That's why you'll never land a man like me,' Richard said smugly.

Jenny grimaced. She recognized flirtation dressed up as feminism. She was being patronized. And yet she liked her domestic omniscience. She liked hearing her name mentioned; it gave her a personality. At school she had sometimes hidden in a locker in case the other girls were talking about her. Once, she had suffered terrible pins and needles but had dug her nails into her hand and persevered because the hockey team were lingering in the changing room discussing who were the most popular members of the class. Her name did not come up until Amanda's voice rose loudly above the rest.

'Of course, the one nobody likes is *Jenny*.' The door was flung open and Jenny stared up at Amanda's triumphant face.

'I told you she hid in here and listened to other peoples' conversations,' she said.

Jenny blinked up at the row of pink-cheeked, mousy-haired girls grinning at her. She stumbled out of the tiny space and said with what dignity she could summon, 'I was not listening. I go in there for some peace and quiet.'

Amanda screwed up her face.

Jenny looked at her with watery reproach. 'I thought you were my friend.'

'I am,' said Amanda, patting her with a strong, sunburned arm. 'You shouldn't worry about what everyone is thinking about you all the time. You should grow up.'

Thirty years later, Jenny still flushed at the memory. The sense of exclusion ran through her like a vein. Yet here she was, married, a hostess, a woman of substance. Her head ached with tiredness and travelling. She unpacked Richard's suitcase, but left her own until the morning. She climbed into bed and drew her legs up beneath her. The voices were dispersing outside.

Minutes later, the door opened and Richard's bulky silhouette moved across the room. He cursed as his foot hit Jenny's suitcase. She was alert as if a burglar were there, but spoke with feigned sleepiness.

'I've put toothpaste on your brush.'

Richard made a series of bathroom noises: sighs, flushing water, a gushing tap. Then he walked round to his appointed side of the bed and took up three quarters of it. Jenny withdrew to her sliver as tightly packaged as if she were in the locker. Richard kissed her, a mix of wine and toothpaste.

'Well done, darling. We're going to have a great time.'

Jenny tentatively stretched out her left leg, registering an option. It was not a night for Richard to heave himself on top of her, but she was prepared for something quick and light. Her hand delved between his thighs and gave the fleshy purses a shake.

'Ah, yup, yup,' sighed Richard.

Voices continued to rise outside on the terrace. It sounded like Toby and Daisy. There was a different kind of murmur from Amanda and Derek's room, lower and graver. From the far end of the house came a woman's shriek.

Richard heaved with laughter, and Jenny lost her grasp.

'Can't compete with that, can we?' whispered Richard. 'Good for Gerry.'

Jenny gave a small offended chuckle. Sex was not a laughing matter to her. It was the reason Richard had married her. If it were merely a saucy sideshow that could be staged by anybody anywhere, what was the point of Jenny? She lay with her arms at her sides, legs together, head turned away. Richard gave her breasts a rub, as if towelling her dry, then turned his back on her.

'We'll have another shot in the morning, shall we, darling? When the coast is clear.' He chortled again and within minutes was snoring peacefully.

Six

Amanda

The warm dawn brought a new palette to the landscape. The pink wash had gone; the sky was blue, the earth was green. Amanda swung her legs over her side of the bed decorously pulling down her bunched-up nightdress. She was self-conscious about exposed flesh since she and Derek had given up sex. Her sleeping husband rolled towards her full of a yearning which would pass when his eyes opened and memory returned.

Amanda tiptoed to the wide-open low bedroom window. The more claustrophobic her existence became, the more she opened windows. At work, she battled with office health and safety regulations in order to open the only latched window in the building; she used coat hangers to break the fastened locks of hotel windows; she risked flu in winter by opening the sash window in her bedroom as far as it would go.

'I was always an outdoor girl,' she explained sheepishly to

Derek. But his invalidity had made her virtually alpine. She leaned out of the window devouring the soft Provence air, tinted with lavender and pine. The landscape was astonishingly still; the breeze glided through the leaves without disrupting them.

The bedroom looked out onto the front courtyard. Amanda hitched herself out of the window and stepped onto the flagstones. This would be her hour of solitude. She picked a stalk of lavender from one of the urns and held it to her nose. Then she crumbled the dry tips in her fingers. She looked back at the sleeping house which would soon bustle with conflicting personalities and wishes, and walked away from it to the dusty drive lined with cypress trees.

In the distance, she saw a figure zigzagging along the main road. The figure turned into the drive. It moved oddly in springy stop-starts. It was a woman jogging. It was Jenny.

Amanda sighed. The art of human cohabitation lies in subtle avoidance. The shared bathroom is a metaphor for group relationships. One needs an intuitive sense of other peoples' daily rhythms so you can arrange your own differently. Amanda had tried to stake her claim as the early riser.

She also felt the natural irritation a woman feels seeing another woman exercising or eating too few calories. It can only be a rebuke. The counter-attack is to sit ostentatiously still or tear into a slice of cake.

Jenny gave a little wave as she approached, then swung

her elbows and exhaled in a series of whistles. Her blonde hair was an untidy mound behind a band and she was wearing a tracksuit stained with damp patches. Amanda crossed her arms over her nightdress and yawned.

'Hi.'

'Hiyayaya.' Jenny bounced on the spot. 'Woah. Phewer. I need to get my breath back.'

People either have adult or childish faces, regardless of their age. Amanda smiled at the sight of her school friend's familiar set of features which were anxiously pretty. The grid of criss-crosses round her eyes and forehead looked as if they had been drawn onto a twelve-year-old's face.

'How is Derek?' asked Jenny. 'Is he OK? Sleeping?'

Amanda nodded. She was used to answering sympathetic questions about Derek. Often people asked her in front of him, in case he could not answer for himself. The couple were objects of pity. That was their assigned role. It did not particularly suit Amanda's cool personality, but circumstances not character turned out to be destiny.

'Do you get time to work out?' asked Jenny, wiping the drops of sweat from the end of her nose. Her assumption that Amanda's life was restricted was partly true and well meant, so Amanda forced herself not to bristle. She had learned to be gracious, to blame nobody.

'Sure, there's a gym at work. And I love walking, if I get the chance.'

'Oh, that's the same as Richard. It probably means you like thinking. When you run you don't think.' Jenny looked around, her hands on her narrow hips. 'So what exactly is your job, Amanda? What do you actually do?'

'It's very straightforward, I advise people on the best way to—'

'I can hear Emily. Yes, that's her, looking for her breakfast, I should think. I had better . . .'

'Of course,' said Amanda. 'You go in. I'll just stay here for a bit.'

Jenny looked pointedly at Amanda's nightdress, and then walked off.

She thinks I'm eccentric, mused Amanda. Oh well, it will give her something to talk about with Richard. She walked back to the window and vaulted into the bedroom.

Derek was propped up with pillows reading a book about the Tour de France. He had grown interested in sport as his limbs wasted.

This was not the determination of the disabled; he had no wish to prove himself in marathons, to win the praise of self-consciously caring television sports presenters. He had merely reached an age where he enjoyed being an armchair sports fan.

'I'm sure you're allowed to use the door,' he said fondly.

Amanda laughed holding her husband's gaze for a full ten seconds. This was a kind of measurement of their marriage.

When Amanda was frustrated or restless she did not look into Derek's eyes, but made do with tight smiles and solicitous enquiries. But for now, there was equilibrium between the couple. She respected him and sometimes remembered that she loved him.

'I got caught out,' she said, bending over the low chest of drawers to take out her clothes from one drawer and Derek's from another. 'I met Jenny on her run. She must have already been up for an hour.'

'I heard her a long time before that,' said Derek, lifting an arm behind his head so that the dark tuft of hair in his armpit showed. 'She was talking to a man outside, don't know who.'

'You must have been dreaming,' said Amanda kindly. 'You were fast asleep.'

She picked up a flannel and went to the basin to rinse it out. She turned one tap and then the other, but both were dry.

'I can't make this—'

'It may be the stopcock, give me a minute and I'll have a look,' said Derek lowering himself unsteadily onto the floor, his limbs trembling with the effort.

'No, don't do that, Derek. Stop, you'll injure yourself,' said Amanda. Her use of his name was a signal that their pleasant intimacy had passed.

There was a knock on the door and both turned to look.

'Jenny sent me to tell you that the water isn't working.' It was Richard's voice. 'We are on the phone to Madame Arnout, so should get it sorted out tout de suite.'

'Do come in,' called Amanda. 'We're both decent.'

A pause. 'Well, that's all I had to say. Bloody French plumbing . . . Sorry about that. We'll try to get it sorted out, so just sit tight in there.'

Derek was balancing himself with one arm on the bed. He screwed up his face at Amanda and she felt a fountain of laughter rising inside her – another sign of good will between them.

'Right,' she said. Jenny wished to imprison them in their room. Were the other guests also under bedroom arrest?

'There's always the window,' whispered Derek as Amanda pushed her shoulder towards him for support.

Half an hour later came the popping sound of a small car negotiating the bumps on the lane. Amanda got up from the chair where she had been reading a book of Sherlock Holmes stories found on the shelf and looked out of the window. A smartly dressed woman with a cigarette in one hand knocked on the door and hummed as she waited. Jenny and Richard appeared with the courteous sour-faced air of dissatisfied consumers. It was the same expression you saw at airports, car-hire desks and restaurants. It said, 'We are bloody annoyed, but we are being British about it and not making an undue fuss.'

'We have children in the house and absolutely cannot do without water,' said Jenny tearfully.

'All right, Jenny, leave this to me,' said Richard his wine vat of a chest rolling towards the Frenchwoman. 'We need this sorted out and we need it fixed now. I'm already looking at a reduction in the cost of this holiday, which is top end of the market.'

Madame Arnout sucked in her cheeks and stubbed out her cigarette.

'You have the button? For the pilot light?'

'I have searched for the pilot light,' said Richard firmly as if that proved it did not exist.

'Excuse me,' said Madame Arnout, pushing past him. Richard followed her suspiciously. A few seconds later there was a grunt from inside.

'Ah, I see. I didn't look there. My apologies.'

'It was totally hidden,' said Jenny loyally.

Madame Arnout emerged from the house.

'Shall I paint it a bright colour in the manner of your speed cameras?' she asked politely, delving into her small handbag for her cigarette packet.

'Ha! Touché! Quite right. I feel like an idiot,' said Richard, holding the driver's door open for her.

'What a dickhead,' whispered Derek encouragingly at his wife.

'No, he said he was sorry; that was sweet,' she replied, her eyes fixed on the window.

An exasperated, privately educated voice hit the couple like a laser from the other direction.

'Can we have a shower now? I can't start the day without one.'

'Syrie,' mouthed Amanda.

'Does she realize it isn't a power shower?' asked Derek.

Amanda winked at him and pulled a green cotton shift dress over her head.

'I had better get going with breakfast,' she said. 'Come when you're ready.'

Amanda was not shy, but she braced herself for company as she walked into the kitchen. Derek's physical demands meant that they tended to do things on their own. She was aware that she had developed masculine traits in compensation. It was her job to carry the luggage and push to the front of queues and buy traveller's cheques. But she also had to remember that successful marriages required a balance of power. She sought areas in which to defer to her husband, she cultivated weakness. Derek was good at crossword puzzles and television quizzes. She had taught herself to poke him in the ribs and cry, 'How on earth did you know that?'

But for the moment, she was the ambassador for her marriage and the breakfast organizer.

Or, as it turned out, kitchen assistant. Jenny was carrying a tray of warm croissants from the oven to the table on the terrace. Her bottom twitched from cheek to cheek with concentration.

'Ah, Amanda, you're back!' she exclaimed, as if Amanda had snuck off on a break. 'Could you possibly get some knives out of the second drawer? There' – she jerked her head. 'Oh, and some condiments.'

Amanda fell in with the preparations without fuss. There were those who waited and those who were waited upon, and they were not to be confused.

Half an hour later, Syrie appeared, flipping her wet hair off her face. She was wearing a virtually see-through white cotton silk kaftan, her breasts surging forwards like rockets.

'Ah, croissants. Fabulous,' she said, easing herself into a chair. 'I can't start the day without breakfast.'

Jenny blinked at her, the hand clutching the bread knife suspended in mid-air.

Amanda folded her arms and sucked in her cheeks to prevent a grin forming. She knew Jenny was running through the list of necessities to start the day and baulking at the likelihood that sex was one of them. Although Amanda had not seen Jenny for ten years or so, she could still read her very well. Jenny's character was fundamentally the same as it had been in childhood: good-naturedness tinged with pique, cleanliness, anxiety, romanticism, slyness, yearning, bewilderment. All these traits were now present in Jenny's transparent face.

'Have you seen my husband?' she said, as if Syrie might be hiding him in her kaftan.

'I think he is outside by the car,' said Amanda, in a deep amused voice. She was enjoying this distraction from her contained life. It was usually Derek who was the source of concern. 'Shall I go and see?'

Richard was examining his golf bag, his heavy face complacent with concentration.

'What's your handicap?' asked Amanda.

'Oh, all over the place, don't get much of a chance to play. About twenty.' He straightened up. 'Are you a golfer?'

'No. Derek used to—'

'Pity. The most frustrating game in the world, but you wouldn't want to do without it. It's no good watching golf, you have to play.'

Amanda liked his direct response. Others might have attempted an artful gloss. They would have said Derek was better off without it. Ruefulness was one of the many tools for dealing with the disabled. The pretence that the life of the able bodied was not as great as it was made out to be. But Richard had used precisely the right word: pity.

He pulled down the boot of the car with large arms that were too thick and strong to be called flabby, but which were undefined by muscle. His stomach, exposed as his polo shirt rode up, was made of the same flesh. Derek, who had been fitter and finer skinned was now more womanly in the looseness of his skin. Amanda shut her eyes to prevent unfavourable comparisons. She was a middle-aged woman. She was an investment adviser. Why was she eyeing this man up so lewdly?

'You any good at flowers?' asked Richard shyly. 'I reckon it's the lavender that smells so good, but there may be something else. I've smelt it in my parents' garden.'

'It's jasmine.' Amanda smiled. Richard was offering her a rational explanation for her momentary trance. How sweet of him.

'Richaaaaard,' Jenny wailed from the kitchen. 'Your croissants are here waiting. Richaaaard.'

'Ah, that's the mating call.' Richard put his hands on his hips, emphasizing his heavy trunk and almost comically short legs. 'It means grub's on the table. Let's go in.'

The group at the table had multiplied. It now included Emily, her face hidden by hair, her elbows jutting at right angles over her bowl of cereal. Toby and Daisy were sitting next to her with the traumatized air of teenagers woken before midday. Gerry was next in the row with the showered complexion and slicked-back hair of a self-congratulatory, sexually active middle-aged man.

'Ha, Goldilocks and the bears, eh, Emily?' said Richard, ruffling his daughter's hair.

'Does Emily know about Goldilocks?' asked Syrie carrying two cups of coffee to the table.

'It must be out of print. I mean it's not exactly relevant to a child's experience now, is it?'

'Well, hang on,' said Richard, winking at Amanda. 'I don't remember bears living next door even when *I* was a child.'

Amanda laughed. She liked Richard's refusal to take offence. She was accustomed to heightened sensitivity towards others' feelings. Of course Derek made jokes, sometimes good jokes and often at his own expense, but that was all part of putting a brave face on it. She warmed to this climate of robustness. And Richard had addressed his joke to her, not to Jenny who was crashing trays about in the oven. Amanda's colleagues sought her out for advice and good judgement, but not for humour. There was not much hilarity in a tax return.

'Will Derek want croissants or cereal? Or I can fry up some bacon,' panted Jenny, her face glowing from the heat of the oven.

'Oh, he doesn't eat much.' Amanda shrugged, feeling a row of sympathetic eyes turning towards her.

'I'm here,' said Derek quietly from his wheelchair in the doorway. 'And a croissant would be lovely, thank you.'

Something Amanda had noticed, in the balancing of life's

accounts, was that personal misfortune was tempered by a fund of general timid goodwill. So she was not altogether surprised when Daisy jumped up, causing a puppyish ripple of midriff over her jeans, and kissed Derek on the top of his head.

'I'll fetch you a croissant, just stay there,' she said, then clapped her hand over her mouth.

Derek beamed at her. 'Well, that's a very pleasant way to start the day.'

'It's going to be hot, hot, hot,' sighed Syrie, and Gerry raised his eyebrows at her with crude expectation.

Oh, really, thought Amanda. Sex was the fool's gold of our age. Here was an intelligent, powerful man reduced to a smutty adolescent. Life was a grown-up business that should be conducted with dignity. Sexual pleasure was a hall of mirrors, mischievous and mocking. She began clearing the plates as Jenny banged the oven door shut in her own gesture of reproach.

'I'm going to work on my tan.' Syrie yawned.

'Swimming, Em?' said Toby.

There was a general clattering of chairs.

'Why don't I drive to the market?' said Richard, clearly nervous of a directionless morning. 'The hire car's arrived. Might be an idea if one of us gets used to it.'

'I'll come with you,' said Amanda quickly.

A group provides cover for marital sleights of hand. Amanda knew she should have checked with Derek, whose health wavered daily within diminishing margins. It was not only his health, but his happiness which she felt was her responsibility. He might have liked a trip to the market, but it was so complicated to take him anywhere. And like all carers Amanda was alert to opportunities for slipping the leash.

Richard held the car door open for her and she settled herself into the passenger seat, shifting the levers to adapt it to her frame. She studied the map, affecting ease to disguise her sudden shyness. This was not her place, this was not her husband. Richard was too big for the car and his oak-like legs were squeezed together to avoid the gears. He plonked an arm across the back of Amanda's seat in order to reverse out and she crouched forward in response.

'Sorry, have you got enough room there?' murmured Richard. Amanda nodded gaily and leant back. She felt the back of her neck touch solid flesh and bounced forward again.

Unfamiliarity was a peculiar state. There was a heightened alertness and self-consciousness that could only be resolved by patient time or impatient sex. Amanda wanted to drape herself over this man's chest, to nestle her head into his neck, to tuck herself into him.

'If we turn left, then right, we should get on the main road,' she said, tracing her manicured finger across the map. She shook her head to clear it of its wandering fantasies.

'Are you cold? This air conditioning . . .' said Richard. Amanda felt the shawl of his concern. People were wrong. The fact that he was a businessman did not make him inconsiderate. On the contrary, he paid attention to detail. And, Amanda mused, he was capable of deep emotion. His vehemence towards the Algerian had only been protectiveness: he looked after those he loved. The notion of being looked after made Amanda's eyelids flicker with surprise.

Amanda was not mad about holidays. Apart from the difficulties of travelling with Derek, the extra forms and different entrances and dependency on strangers, there was the disproportionate cost. You budgeted during the year then, whoosh, three months' worth gone in a week. Holidays were the black hole in domestic expenditure and wasteful for companies. When you needed something signed, you could bet your bottom euro that person was on holiday. She sighed over the emails that pinged back to say that so and so was out of the office for the week ending ... or not ending. Business travel was quite a different thing, calm, purposeful, efficient. Amanda liked glancing up from her laptop through the plane window, registering mountains or sea or clouds, and knowing that she had passed over a country without incident.

But she was not a joyless person. There were rewarding holiday moments and one of them was feeling the sun on her back and an unfamiliar smell of dusty soil, fresh air and fruit, and keeping in step with the bulky man alongside her.

'What do you think? Melons? Grapes?' said Richard deferentially.

'Let's pick up the heaviest things last,' Amanda replied. 'We'll start with the meats, then bread, then fruit. And you said a present for Jenny?'

'Yuuh,' said Richard.

'It's not Harvey Nichols, here, is it? I don't suppose it's very romantic to give your wife sausages for her birthday.' There's a fabric stall over there. Those pretty blue and yellow napkins are jolly. Or a pot?'

'Are you any good at wrapping?' asked Richard hopefully.

'No,' said Amanda emphatically. 'My parcels look as if a dog has got hold of them. I don't know why I am so bad at it.'

'It's a skill. But it is one you can live without quite happily. Anything pongy you can see?'

'I wouldn't want to choose perfume for another woman, it's such an intimate thing isn't it?'

'Oh, Jen used to buy it for Virg— Sorry, that's rather bad taste, isn't it? Mustn't mention first wives unless it is practical or sympathetic. Isn't that right?'

Amanda glanced at Richard to see if he were being sardonic, but his face was matter of fact. She noticed he had sleepy dust on his eyelashes, but that was something only a wife could mention.

'Those napkins would be lovely,' she said.

The stallholder was a squat, dark man with thick hair growing on his upper arms and shoulders.

'*Pour vôtre femme?*' His plump arms reached over his display. 'You like?'

'I'm not his wife,' said Amanda.

'*Alors,*' replied the stallholder slyly.

He pulled a dainty lace-edged chemise from a hanger behind him and beckoned to the couple.

'Can't see you in that somehow.' Richard chuckled and Amanda laughed hard, but she thought, Why not?' Am I sexless?

They wandered back to the car, which was wedged between a row of erratically parked, badly dented vehicles in a shady narrow street.

Relationships are built on shared anecdotes, and this was one to bank. Amanda already felt a greater degree of comfort in Richard's presence, which meant she was enjoying his company. As they negotiated their way through small crowds of local cars and holiday makers with no road sense, Amanda exclaimed, 'Look! There's the guy from last night.'

Richard looked round; as he did so the graceful figure of Ahmed crossed behind a group of elderly women in black.

'You sure it was him?'

'Yes, I saw his face.'

The Villa

There was a trickle of sweat on Richard's upper lip. It was already midday and the heat was merciless.

'I suppose he must live round here,' said Richard lamely.

There was a pause. They did not know each other well enough to read the language of silence. Amanda felt depressed, which meant she was missing Derek. Why was she in this car with somebody else's husband? She had no business being here. Selfishness always produced an initial blood-rush followed by a terrible sadness. She thought mournfully of the moments she had been impatient with Derek. When they had to miss the West End musical she had booked on her credit card (incurring extra charges) because Derek had felt lousy and she had said, 'Oh, what does it matter? It doesn't matter at all,' with enough sharpness and avoidance of eye contact to convey both martyrdom and exasperation. Or the time she had left him in his wheelchair at a beauty spot on the South Downs so she could have a quick peek at the valley, but then had kept on walking, faster and faster for miles, and almost an hour had passed before she returned. Derek did not reproach her; he just looked pale and pathetic. Amanda always felt wretched after a break-out and became subdued and strangely clingy. Her dependence on Derek sometimes exceeded his on her. As Amanda and Richard drove back after their shopping trip, she felt weak with relief when the low shape of the villa came into view. But then, as soon as she reached the door, she felt sorry that a morning alone with Richard was over.

Seven

'There you are.' Jenny waved from the terrace, her effusive welcome full of reproach. She was crouched on a sun lounger as if in the middle of a stomach exercise. A stack of magazines lay by her small, manicured feet. She was wearing a blue flowery bathing costume but reached for a sarong which somehow became tangled in her sun visor as she threw the material round her back.

'Did you get lost?'

'Hello, darling,' said Richard. 'Please don't abuse the workers.'

'I've only just sat down myself,' said Jenny baring her little white teeth in a weird grimace. 'What have you bought?'

Richard did not answer. He saluted the rest of the group and moved like a walking tree to the bedroom to put his bathing trunks on.

Amanda started to unpack the bags in the kitchen.

'I ran after you with a list, but you didn't see me,' said Jenny, snatching food from the nearest bag and carrying it to the fridge.

'No, we didn't. I'm sorry,' said Amanda calmly.

'I fell over and hurt my knee,' said Jenny, plaintively pointing at a graze.

'I'm sorry,' repeated Amanda. She remembered a school geography trip where the coach had left without Jenny. Why was that? Oh yes, she had been to the lavatory and the coach had left. Amanda had swayed up the aisle and told a harassed-looking teacher that Jenny was not on board. The girls kneeled along the back row and laughed and cheered as Jenny's pert face came into view. After they had picked her up, Jenny sat in the seat in front of Amanda, her face a tragic mask. She had refused to speak to Amanda for a week. That was the trouble with Jenny; her skin was as thin as a butterfly's wing. What is appealing sensitivity in the young is inexcusable egotism in middle age.

'Sorry you hurt your knee,' said Amanda coldly.

She poured herself a glass of water and took it outside. The sunbathers were arranged in a tableau of flesh. Gerry was flung back in repose, his tight Speedo trunks mocked by a paunch and a slightly withered-looking pale chest. His face, in the bright light had a grey tint to it. On the next sun lounger, Syrie posed, her legs on one side, an s-shape of youthful contours, her skin like fawn satin. She invited the exclamation: 'What is she doing with him?' That was why she was with him.

Daisy had thrown herself on the grass in generational

solitude, a mini-disc player attached to her ears. She had a lovely body, still chubby with childhood, marked only by imprints from the ground. Toby floated on his back in the pool, his still newly minted flesh tight across his torso. He started as the boulder-like form of his father crashed into the pool, displacing half the water. Amanda laughed and sat cross-legged next to Derek, who was clothed and upright on a hall chair. She was glad he had his shirt on. He had thus excused himself from being revealed as a biology text-book illustration of the phases of ageing. She took his hand and kissed it, and he looked at her with searching, chlorine-coloured eyes.

'How was your morning?'

'Oh, hot. I missed you,' she whispered.

Derek inhaled hoarsely and then screwed his face up against the sun. Amanda had not meant to frighten him with guilty outbursts of affection. She released his hand.

'Have you been in the pool yet?'

'A bit later,' he said. He did not need to say that he needed her assistance and would prefer to conduct the ordeal without a crowd of witnesses.

'Sure,' said Amanda.

'Won't you go in?'

'Oh, no. I'll wait.'

'Are you coming in, Amanda?' bellowed Richard, surfacing at the deep end like a blue whale.

Amanda hesitated.

'Oh, all right, hang on.'

She fetched her gym-mistress navy-blue costume and dived in. She was a strong swimmer, with an athletic crawl. She sliced her way through the water stopping short of Richard at the far end. She held on to the side, to stop her lower body from floating towards him.

'I'm coming in toooo,' announced Jenny, lowering herself down the ladder at the shallow end. 'Woosh, oooh, it's cold.'

'It isn't cold, Jenny, if this is cold...' replied Richard sinking below the surface so that his hair floated between Amanda's fingers like seaweed. She pushed his head away, laughing as a route from awkwardness.

Jenny's head bobbed towards them, in studious breast-stroke, her chin thrust upwards. As she reached the deep end she wrapped her arms and legs around Richard, chuckling flirtatiously. Amanda returned to the shallow end with a thrashing backstroke and pulled herself out of the pool.

'Oh, don't get out,' said Richard trying to manoeuvre his wife, who was floating sideways in his arms, away from him as if he was launching a dinghy.

Amanda affected not to hear and dried herself harshly with a towel. She was too old for these games. Too old and too married.

*

Supper al fresco was an oddly formal affair. A group of this size fell naturally into the habits of the country house. Having spent the day with each other, near enough naked, they withdrew to their rooms with only the sounds of competing plumbing, low whispers, some inevitable grunting from Gerry and Syrie's quarters and furniture being scraped across the floor from Jenny and Richard's. Toby and Daisy stayed outside laughing and splashing. Emily's commentary as she moved in and out of the house was more or less continuous. Amanda's head ached from the sun and the sustained company and she joined Derek in an invalid's slumber, with the shutters drawn. Ill health was, after all, the mark of her private world.

Then, suddenly, at eight, they were all outside in a change of clothes, the women made-up, the men shaved. Gerry's complexion was the most vivid, giving his face a slightly expanded, bloated appearance. Jenny was wearing a tight sundress, with the price tag hanging jauntily down her back, her blonde hair rolling over the top of her head like a wave. Her manufactured mixed perfume fought with the more gentle odour of the warm, lavender dusk and the aroma of sex, given off by Syrie, which everyone recognized, in the same way people knew the unmistakable scent of cannabis.

Both Jenny and Amanda had the distracted air of women in charge of the food. Their eyes scanned the table for missing elements and their conversation was cut short with trips to and from the kitchen. Jenny had been careful in her pre-holiday conversations to stress to her guests that they would all muck in with meals, but this could only be achieved with consultation or stubborn neglect. Jenny was too anxious to display her domestic accomplishments for this to happen and Amanda could not stand by and do nothing. There was no such thing as feminism on holiday. The men were excused chores by virtue of their gender, Daisy because of her youth and Syrie because of her work in the bedroom. That was the implicit understanding.

Drinks were poured and tongues were loosened. The conversation repeated the pattern of the first night: the men's voices loud and unwilling to give way, the women's voices trickling through the slabs of male oratory.

'So when are we going to get you lot out?' said Richard jabbing his fork at Gerry.

'Not while you lot are led by a lot of prancing nonentities,' Gerry shouted back.

'Well then, you'll run the economy into the ground. Let's look at all the stealth taxes and the politically correct employment rights bollocks. What about the minimum wage? Forget it, we'll relocate in Bangladesh, we will,' yelped Richard.

'I don't think I should like it in Bangladesh,' sighed Jenny.

'What does everyone think will happen in the American election? I'm sooo annoyed that it isn't being covered properly on television here,' said Syrie, addressing only the men.

'Who are the candidates?' Jenny asked, cocking her head.

Syrie caught as many eyes round the table as she could.

'Sorry? What did you say?'

Jenny blinked.

'I just asked who is standing against the president?'

Syrie guffawed.

'I can't believe your question.'

'There is life outside politics, Syrie,' said Derek mildly. 'We are not all as committed as you. Very happy to let you run the country, or indeed the world, on our behalf. Grateful for it. This is marvellous cheese. Did you get it from the market?'

Jenny glanced furtively at Syrie. She was frowning. So she doesn't use Botox, Jenny thought.

There are many hours of awkwardness and irritation during a holiday with friends but there are compensating passages of sheer delight, usually a few bottles down the line. The conversation was punctuated by laughter and eyes were glinting in the light of the guttering candles. The plates of food were piled carelessly, losing ground to the increasing number of empty bottles picked up and examined for dark or light liquid, and to overflowing ashtrays. Emily tried out different laps for comfort, pulling at adult features as if they were Play-Doh. Then she lost interest and wandered back to the house.

Drink affected the members of the group in slightly different ways. Gerry was alternately argumentative and mawkish, finally banging his fist on the table and shouting through tears that the war must be won because 'Kids are our future. Syrie's kids.' The laughter and simulated vomiting that greeted him did not penetrate, although Syrie shrugged distastefully and Daisy's hand shook as she lit a cigarette. (Toby slipped his palm into her other hand.) Jenny grew more flirtatious and teasing, years of office parties manifesting themselves in cries for a round of strip poker or the who-would-you-sleep-with game. Richard was a benign, sober drunk, the kind who would eventually keel over like a felled tree.

Amanda reminded herself that it was her role to match wine with water and she kept an account of her consumption. She was perfectly steady when she lent Derek an arm to help him to bed before his nervous system deteriorated in front of everybody.

The difference Amanda experienced was a kind of heightened athleticism. She stretched her arms high above her head and rolled her ankles. She felt as if she could run, or jump or fly.

'What about a quick evening swim, Amanda!'

'Oh, yes!'

She turned to go inside and fetch her costume, but Derek would be sleeping. Or worse, he would be awake. She stood poised, as if on the starting line.

'I'm all right in this,' she said half to herself. It was dark, no one could see. 'I'm coming in!'

She pulled off her dress, jumped into the pool and was immediately submerged by the warm, night water. She could hear muffled applause. What was this? Amanda the exhibitionist? She flicked her legs, as if wearing flippers, propelling herself under water across the length of the pool. Her mind was as weightless as her body; she was perfectly free.

Then she was joined by a dark submarine of a body. Richard touched her waist as he passed her. She waved back an acknowledgement, her hand brushing against his flapping swimming trunks. How long could they hold their breath? She wished the pool was as deep as Loch Ness. They came up for air at the same time, their legs tangled, their bodies apart, their faces shocked.

'What's going on over there?' came a peevish voice from the terrace. 'Richard? Madame Arnout is here. Come and say hello.'

Richard and Amanda pulled themselves out of the water and walked with guilty insouciance towards the burning ember of a cigarette which led to the rest of Madame Arnout.

'Please continue your pleasure.' The long hand waved. 'It is the place to be, in the pool. It has been so hot today. Hot enough for you English?'

Amanda groped along the paving stones for her dress, her hair dripping uncomfortably onto her bra.

'I'll just go in and get dry,' she said flatly. 'Excuse me.'

She passed Emily inside, sitting upright on a wooden chair, like a judge.

'Hello, Emily,' she said.

'You've been in the pool,' said Emily, sternly. 'Does Ahmed know?'

'Ahmed?'

'The pool guy. He told me he puts chemicals in there at night. That's what he was doing when Daddy tried to arrest him for abucting me.'

'Abducting. Your daddy didn't really think that. He was just worried about you.'

'Ahmed wouldn't steal me. He doesn't have anywhere to take me. He would prefer to live with us.'

'When did he tell you this?'

'Tomorrow he told me. Oh, silly me, not tomorrow, it couldn't be tomorrow, it was today.'

'Was Ahmed here today?'

'Of course he was. He lives here.'

'Where Emily? Where does he live? Did he show you?'

'No, he showed me some plates he'd made. He's a really good painter. He's going to teach me to paint. With proper paint and not just stupid crayons.'

'Amanda? Is that you?' A tired voice came from her bedroom.

'Yes, darling, just coming. Emily, shall I take you to bed? Do you want to get on my back?'

Emily folded her small golden arms, which were covered in fine blonde hair. She recoiled into her own warmth and dryness.

'No, thank you. I can go by myself.'

She rose and walked lightly down the corridor. Amanda gazed after her. The adult quality of childhood was a surprise to her. Just as the childish quality of adulthood appalled her. Emily was a model of self-possession. Therein lay her innocence.

Amanda's head was full of snakes.

She went into the bedroom and towel-dried her hair roughly until the strands formed a hard mass. She looked at Derek, who blinked back at her.

'You look lovely,' he said.

His thin chest rose and fell beneath the tangled bedclothes, infused with body heat. It was an invalid's bed. Amanda adapted her gestures for this self-made sanatorium: she started folding clothes; she plumped up the pillows and carried a glass of water to the side table.

'Can't you sleep?' she asked quietly. Derek reached out his hand to touch her face and she grabbed it in mid-air.

'You must try to sleep,' she said, placing it back under the sheet.

'Will you come to bed?' Derek asked, his face drawn and anxious.

Amanda glanced at the window and sighed.

'Yes, I'm coming to bed now.'

She put on her nightdress and scrubbed her teeth, staring blankly at herself in the mirror, smeared her face in cream and walked past the window to her side of the bed. She switched out the light.

'The woman,' said Madame Arnout outside, following Richard's glum stare, 'in her white dress. The lady with the light. Who is that? Like Lady Jane Grey. To the Tower, no?'

'Lady with the lamp, you mean,' said Jenny shrilly. 'Florence Nightingale. Looking after sick men. That's Amanda.'

Amanda had become practised at lying very still at night, her breathing the faintest whisper. Derek was more restless because of the inactivity of his day. They no longer discussed his fearful sweating and moans. There was no solution and probing the nocturnal abyss of his mind gave no comfort. Illness was a lonely state. Amanda dreamed of swimming, first across the pool and then in an ocean without location. She was dimly aware that she could not swim for ever and that there was no land in sight. She was filled with an infinite peacefulness.

Then something hit her face with colossal force. Derek was in a minor spasm, his arm swinging across her cheek like a boat's boom. She threw herself out of reach and crouched, panting, by the side of the bed.

'I k-choo, Mnda,' cried Derek, his body moving in every direction, sub-human, mythological.

Amanda's heart thundered, but she let out a long 'Shhh', like a radiator being drained. 'Derek, shhhhhhhhhhh. You're OK.'

He pulled his wayward limbs towards his trunk as if trying to fasten his body down. His hair was streaming with sweat.

'Shhhhhhhhhhhhhhhhhhhhh. It's OK, OK.'

Finally he was quiet. Amanda directed her trembling hand towards his shoulder. It twitched in rejection.

She continued to crouch in the suffocating heat. She turned towards the window narrowing her eyes at a distant light from the shore. A home? A lighthouse? God? When it was safe and her heartbeat had quietened, she crept back beneath the sheets. This was her life. Hopelessness.

By morning however, the covers of their relationship were back on.

'Will you be leaving by the window or the door?' asked Derek cheerfully as Amanda helped dress him.

'I'm going straight to the kitchen,' she replied. 'I'm starving. I have to get to those croissants before Syrie wolfs them all.'

'God knows, that girl needs them; she's coming in from a night shift,' said Derek.

Amanda laughed, expelling the last vestiges of fear.

'I'll bring some back for you.'

She opened the door a crack, looked both ways, then jogged towards the kitchen. Jenny was sitting alone at the table in a tracksuit and full make-up, with a cup of coffee and several sheets of paper.

'Hello, you're up,' she said, sucking her pencil. 'I'm just making a shopping list. I thought I'd send Richard off early so it doesn't take the whole day.'

Amanda looked at the pile of croissants on the worktop. Could she slip some into her pockets behind Jenny's back?

'Mind if I make some coffee?'

'Let me make it.' Jenny jumped up. Amanda flapped her arms in resignation. This woman was like a dragon guarding the kitchen treasure. Holidays were like *The Lord of the* bloody *Rings*: just one obstacle after another. Everyone humouring each other, while plotting their escape.

'Is Emily still asleep? I had a chat with her last night. She'd seen Ahmed again. You know, the man we . . . um . . . chatted to, that first evening?'

Jenny tapped her foot as the kettle billowed steam.

'Yes, I know. He's employed by Madame Arnout. Emily and I have rather adopted him. He's an artist, actually. I find we understand each other. Which is more than I can say about those sex fiends down the corridor.'

Amanda folded her arms, amused.

'Are you talking about the member of Her Majesty's Government?' she asked.

Jenny pulled up her tracksuit bottoms in a gesture of indignation.

'I should imagine he's too shagged out to do any governing,' she said.

'Who's too shagged out?' came a voice from behind them.

Jenny and Amanda took a step towards each other in guilty solidarity.

'Oh . . . hi, Syrie.'

'Do you have a problem with our sex life?' said Syrie, who was wearing pants and a little vest, her nipples standing out like darts, her hair pornographically tousled.

'No!' said the other women, shaking their heads at the sheer improbability of the proposition.

'Good,' said Syrie, catching sight of the croissants. 'Hey, I need sustenance. The thing with older guys is there's so much more foreplay.' She stuffed a croissant into her clitoris-coloured mouth. 'You OK discussing sex?' she said as she munched. 'I don't want to freak you out or anything.'

'I'm just trying to make a list,' said Jenny faintly.

Amanda felt suddenly protective towards her old friend. Here she was, on the eve of her birthday, being assaulted by sexual triumphalism. It was intimidation. It was politics.

'Actually, you're interrupting our early morning, hot lesbian session,' she said drily.

'Whatshru?' choked Syrie.

'She's joking!' yelped Jenny.

Amanda shrugged. 'OK, maybe not. You shag away, Syrie. Good luck to you. It's sometimes a necessary substitute for conversation or compassion. It certainly gets you out of your share of housework.'

Syrie's face fell. 'Look, sorry, I didn't mean ... anything I can do?'

'You could hand round the croissants,' replied Amanda.

Her rebuke had been administered, she thought, perfectly calmly and professionally, yet she felt a prickle of unease. She hoped nobody would examine it closely. Syrie had played her sexual card, but she had responded with the martyr's ace. Derek's disability would now cast a pall.

The three women navigated themselves cautiously round the kitchen carrying plates and mugs and kitchen cloths. Jenny hummed snatches from *Chicago*, Syrie wondered aloud if she might walk to the village to find an English newspaper. Amanda almost offered to go with her, but thought better of it.

'It'll be awfully hot,' she said, scrubbing at a patch of congealed tomato ketchup. Her shoulders relaxed at the sound of men's voices. Domestic relief, sexual tension.

Richard and Gerry pushed competitively through the door.

'Morning, girls!' called Richard.

'Morning, coven!' Gerry smirked. His forehead was glistening, either from the shower or the morning heat.

'Hey!' said Syrie, wrapping an arm round his neck. 'Do you want to walk with me to get a paper?'

133

Gerry gave a whistling sigh. 'I thought I might just lie by the pool this morning. This heat is draining. Feel a bit sick actually.'

'Well, you're fun,' said Syrie folding her arms. 'Come on, let's *do* something.'

'OK, OK, OK. Can I have some breakfast first?'

'You just said you felt sick.'

Jenny handed Gerry a cup of coffee and a plate. 'You might feel better if you have something to eat.'

Gerry held her eye gratefully. 'That's what I need, a bit of mothering.'

'Uh oh,' said Syrie, moving aerobically from one foot to another. 'When a man starts calling for his mother, I am out of here.'

Gerry's face shimmered in the heat, like an oasis.

'Right. Let's go. I'll just get some money. Are you going to get dressed, Syrie?'

Syrie planted her talons on her rolling hips.

'I am dressed. This is what I'm wearing today. A problem?'

'You look great,' said Richard.

They watched the couple leave, Gerry seeming to pull his body along, as Syrie danced ahead of him like a lightweight boxer.

'That girl has a lot of energy,' said Richard as he swallowed his coffee.

Amanda smiled indulgently. She was less affronted by Syrie's egotism now that Richard was around. She was used to the self-conscious good looks of the younger girls in the office. It was part of the environment. And whatever turbulence they caused, in the end, they stood or fell by their competence with balance sheets.

It was Jenny who felt the head winds more directly, who had to deal with a husband's discontent. But then, thought Amanda, you reap what you sow.

'There'll be an early harvest at this rate,' said Richard.

Amanda started.

'What?'

'This heat. Good for the grapes but I'm not sure about the rest. The farmers will have to get going.'

'I didn't know you were so expert on land management,' said Amanda.

'Oh, I'm a country boy.'

'Didn't you know?' said Jenny. 'He's Gabriel Oat.'

'Oaks,' said Amanda.

'Oats,' replied Jenny politely.

Amanda waited for Richard to authenticate her reading of Hardy. Jenny's mouth tightened.

'Too hot for golf, anyway,' said Richard. 'Might do some practice swings on the terrace.'

'You can't, Daddy,' said Emily, who had come in while they

were talking. She looked a tiny, composed figure, clutching a croissant in her clenched hand. 'That's where Ahmed dries out his pots.'

'Hello, little princess,' Richard said, squatting down cravenly before his daughter. 'And who is Ahmed? Is he your imaginary friend?'

'I'm not a princess, I'm Emily.' She sighed, pushing her sticky hand into his face. 'And Ahmed isn't imaginary. He lives here.'

Richard's knees creaked as he pulled himself up.

'Is he the chap . . . ?'

'Yes, he works for Madame Arnout,' said Jenny quickly, clearing the plates from the table. 'He really is Gabriel Oats. Oats,' she repeated for emphasis.

'Who is Gabriel bloody Oats? And who is Ahmed? I mean, I know who he is, but who is he?' asked Richard irritably.

'Poor Richard,' said Jenny, thrusting out her lower lip. 'Poor baby, no one is telling you anything, are they?'

She stood on tiptoe to kiss his neck, in imitation of his daughter. But while daughters can patronize their fathers with impunity, wives cannot.

Richard glared at her. 'Thank you, Jenny. I suppose those sheets of paper are a shopping list. You have that gloating air of a woman determined to spend money. Give them to me.'

Jenny shamefully handed over the list, as if it were soiled homework.

Amanda hoped and dreaded that Richard would ask her to accompany him, but he turned his back on them and stalked off, his hands groping for change in the pockets of his roomy shorts.

In a way, Amanda was pleased to be alone with Jenny. Since she was in the luxurious position of contemplating an affair without committing herself, she could advance tentatively into the married couple's life without attracting suspicion. It was unpleasant to think she was spying on Jenny, but the flicker of wickedness was a novel sensation. Amanda studied Jenny. She was pretty, but slightly tiresome. Her bodily maintenance was transparent: her skin was moist from the use of subscribed face creams, her arms were toned by lifting weights, but sagged under the armpits. She was supported by a scaffolding of exercise and moisture, which lent her a look of vulnerability. It was as if she were pleading for funds to continue the project.

'I must speak to Madame Arnout,' fretted Jenny, 'about booking a restaurant for tomorrow. There's a great one up on the hill, but I don't know about disabled access.' She shot a look at Amanda combining sympathy and reproach.

'We could stay here,' replied Amanda immediately. 'You go, with Richard and the others.'

'Oh, no, we want you there. Richard loves your company,' said Jenny shyly.

Amanda brightened at the compliment despite its curious source.

'I must say, Richard is great fun. He pulls you up, doesn't he? Makes you work harder.'

'Hmm,' said Jenny. 'Bonus-related performance. You can take the man away from the office . . .'

'Out of the office,' corrected Amanda, smiling.

'Yes, that's good.'

Toby wandered into the room, a towel wrapped round his waist.

Jenny glowed at him.

'This is early for you, isn't it? My God, are those hairs on your chest? Not my baby any more.'

'Jenny, you didn't know me when I was a baby,' Toby said sweetly. Was he the only adult present with a sense of family propriety? 'Where's Dad?'

'He's gone to the shops. And I did know you. I fell in love with you at first sight.'

'Whooaah, Oedipus,' said Toby.

Amanda chuckled at the A-level text references and the putting down of Jenny. Why was she being so horrid?

'Another stressed-out day by the pool?' she suggested. Toby gave her a conspiratorial look. The approval of the young was so very flattering. Basking in the endorsement, she took her leave.

'I'll bring Derek out,' she said. Was she making him sound

like a freak show? Her emerging moral ambivalence made her feel seasick.

'I'll put a seat in the shade for him, next to Daisy. She dotes on Derek,' Toby said kindly.

See, see, thought Amanda. Everyone could be made happy. All it took was an alternative pairing off, a holiday reshuffle.

By eleven o'clock the hill was scorched by a Sahara-like heat and the earth began cracking with subsidence. Amanda and Jenny ferried out jugs of iced water which became warm within minutes. The flimsiest clothing pressed against flesh like rubber suiting. The sunbeds were lined up in the sliver of shade to the right of the pool.

'God, this is like Baghdad,' panted Jenny, bent double as she patched up the pink varnish on her toes. Emily wriggled closer to her mother.

'Can I have some of that?' she asked. Jenny applied the brush to her daughter's fingernails.

Richard's shadow fell on them as he stood in front of them like a large, melting ice cream.

'I've put the bags in the kitchen,' he said, his amiable face coloured with jolly scarlet stripes.

Amanda, whose bed was squeezed between Derek and Daisy contracted her stomach and shielded her face with her hand.

'You could do with a swim,' she called out.

'Are you coming in, Daddy?' said Emily, hopping from one foot to the other, her drying nails stretched out flat before her.

'In a minute,' he said. 'I'll just get rid of my clobber.'

'Get in now, Daddy.'

'In a minute.'

'Now, Daddy.'

She gave him a sharp shove, disproportionate to her weight and size. Richard swayed like a tower block on the verge of demolition, then tipped backwards, falling in slow motion into the pool.

'Oh, no!' cried Jenny. 'Your things! Oh, darling.'

Richard floated to the surface, his billowing shorts and shirt like a sail above his body. With some dignity he fished in his pocket and pulled out his dripping wallet and keys, which he placed deliberately on the side of the pool.

'Emily, you naughty girl, you bad, stupid girl,' screeched Jenny.

Emily looked wide-eyed at her mother, and then turned and ran into the house.

'Well,' said Richard, standing waist-deep in the shallows. 'Who will join me?'

Jenny blinked fast and repeatedly.

'Go and fetch Ems,' said Richard, jerking his sodden head.

'It's not bloody funny,' said Jenny, trotting off after her

daughter. The sound of dramatic sobs were already echoing from within.

'Amanda, you look too hot, get in,' called Richard, wading towards her.

Amanda stepped into the glare of Richard's attention. What could she do? She collapsed into the pool, knowing that his arms would rescue her. As he swung her round, she looked at the blur of faces in the distance. Under the water, she pressed her hand against the stump beneath his shorts. They had crossed the line. This was the day they would have sex. This would be the promise of the holiday fulfilled.

It also seemed predestined that consummation would take place in the swimming pool. This had less to do with Amanda's water metaphors than practical opportunity. The distraction was the midday heat and the return of Syrie and Gerry. Gerry complained loudly of sunstroke and took to his room. The sun continued obligingly to sap the strength of each member of the group. By two o'clock, even Emily had crept into the shade of the house, and had fallen asleep diagonally on top of her bed. Jenny peered out at the terrace a couple of times, then retreated to her room with a pile of magazines. Daisy, Toby and Derek went to watch cycling on the television.

'Not my sport, too energetic,' said Richard, finishing off another bottle of beer.

'Oh, I love watching sportsmen in pain,' said Derek cheerfully.

'You wait until next year,' said Daisy, negotiating his wheelchair through the door. 'I'm entering you for the paralympics.'

Amanda gave them a wave from the side of the pool. She knew Derek was happy in their company; she didn't have to feel guilty. This was her sabbatical from guilt. She circled a leg in the water, watching her strong white limb with detachment. She turned her face towards the sun, her eyes closed. Then she felt Richard's body next to her and smelt his beery breath.

'You look as happy as a dolphin,' he said. The thick flubber of his body could be mistaken for a sea lion but, Amanda thought, mammal analogies were best not pursued further. Keeping her eyes closed she turned towards him, felt his hand reach behind her head and the unfamiliar, watery thrust of his tongue in her mouth. It had been so long since she had kissed anybody but her husband that she felt gawky in her technique.

She sensed that the fucking would be easier than the kissing, and so it was. The method for this, considering the obvious difficulties of gravity and water was really quite advanced. Fortunately, Richard was ready from the start, because foreplay would have been tricky and oral sex imposs-ible without drowning. Amanda propped herself up on her arms, and concentrated on stopping her legs from floating too quickly to the surface. There – they had managed it. Richard was inside her, looking gratifyingly amazed. He pulled out leaving a trail of slime that Amanda caught in her fingers.

'Oh, my darling,' he said fondly, returning his cock to his swimming trunks. Then he kissed Amanda again with a quiet kindness that brought tears to her eyes. She swum towards him, wrapping her arms round his shoulders, her legs round his back. This was the fusion of bodies she had so desired. She could not, would not, let go.

Then Richard pushed her away, cursing.

'Oh, Christ, it's that bloody man again, creeping around.'

Amanda splashed wildly in a circle, her heart clattering.

'Where, where is he? Did he see us?'

That was the trouble with adultery. The consequences were so much greater than the action. She stared at Richard as they both ran through the possibilities: it hadn't been Emily; it hadn't been Jenny. It was not a crisis, but it was a warning. They could stop here, now. But once the immediate danger had passed, Richard was already frisky again. He ran his hand down Amanda's thigh.

'We're OK.' He grinned. 'And God, that was nice.'

He got out of the pool and sauntered over to the shade and started doing press-ups, energetically and with sexual pride. Then he threw himself into a deckchair, which collapsed. Amanda laughed hard with pleasure and relief.

'Don't laugh,' said Richard with mock offence. 'I could have injured myself. You know, there's a chap at work, bit of a nerd – spectacles, American. Anyway, he has this special chair which he bought himself. For his back – orthopaedic, or orthodontic, or whatever it's called. So, everyone waits until he goes out to the loo or gets coffee, then they swap the chair for an ordinary one. I watch him mincing up and down outside my office. He puts his glasses down on his desk and stands there, like this, and says: "OK, that is so hilarious. Who has taken my chair? Who has taken my goddamn chair?" Everyone looks surprised and stares at their computers. And he is practically crying: "Who has taken my chair?" It's just so funny. Don't know what made me think of it. I want to fuck you again, Amanda.'

Amanda felt as if she were slipping through her skin. She sat down cross-legged in wonder. Everything was the same, and yet everything was different. She felt better and worse. More herself and less so.

'You're so gorgeous,' said Richard.

He had made her so. She stretched her arms above her head and smiled at him.

There were voices inside the house and minutes later Emily came running out.

'Not fair, that you can stay outside,' she said, hopping across the coal-hot paving stones. 'I want to do what you are doing.'

Amanda and Richard exchanged glances. From now on they had their own secret language, a conspiracy against even

144

a ten-year-old child. Jenny trotted out carrying towels and sun cream. She squinted suspiciously at the sky.

'It is still so hot,' she said accusingly. 'Even inside it is like . . .'

'An oven?' suggested Amanda. She reproached herself. She must stop patronizing Jenny. She should be nicer to her friend now she was screwing her husband. But adultery did not make people nice. It made them cruel. It unleashed a primitive irritation towards anything that stood in the way of their own pleasure. Their own needs were elevated above everybody else's. Amanda's marriage was based on kindness; it seemed a very fragile quality at that moment.

However, she did experience a moment of sorrow when Derek staggered out on his crutches, his face damp with concentration and effort. Yesterday, she would have registered this feeling as pity, but now it had the added weight of shame.

'Are you managing?' she asked, moving swiftly towards him. He held her back with his eyes.

'Much stronger, thank you,' he said, with his customary soft civility. 'I think watching those cyclists has got the muscles working in sympathy. What about driving across country to watch them later in the week?'

'Sure,' said Amanda, thinking, But that's a day away from Richard.

So long as she was in his presence however, she could be a solicitous wife. There was a generosity to her sexual vitality.

She chatted to Toby and Daisy and taught Emily how to do backstroke. She made tea for everybody. She complimented Syrie on her change of dress, made of unsuitable black lycra. Only Jenny made her tense, not so much from guilt as anguish at her claims on Richard: the way she sat on his lap, tucked his T-shirt into his shorts and entertained the group with rambling memories of her pregnancy, which made Amanda think sharply of conception. No, Jenny she could not bear.

The acuity of her feelings shocked her. On the one hand she hardly knew Richard beyond their friendly banter and intense, but brief, sexual intercourse. She did not fool herself that he was her soulmate – simple probability forbade it. So there was no other hand. She was a trained accountant, she dealt with life's realities. Her delirium was more to do with a release within herself. She knew she was behaving out of character and was intrigued by this other self. This is who she might have been.

'How did you two meet?' asked Jenny cosily.

Amanda shook herself.

'What? We? We met here.'

Jenny stared her oddly.

'You met here? Hello?'

'I am afraid to say it was at a firm's do,' prompted Derek protectively. 'Amanda was doing our accounts. She was wearing a long red dress with a sort of band round the top, what do you call that?'

'Halter neck,' said Amanda quickly. 'Sorry, I was miles away.'

'What about you two?'

Jenny brushed some crumbs from her lap.

'Oh, same sort of thing. Social.'

'A very social office,' teased Toby as he strode past carrying a pile of pool toys.

'Toby!' said Jenny, hurt.

'Sorry. Faux pas,' he said, and then shouted, 'Ems, I've got your whale and diving rings. Are you coming in?'

'You don't have to shout,' said Jenny in nervous reproach.

'But there's no one around,' said Toby. 'There's just us, all alone, miles from anywhere. Cool place for a murder.'

'Is there going to be a murder?' said Emily, dancing out of the bushes, and jumping into the pool. 'Who's going to be murdered?'

'You, if you don't keep your voice down,' snapped Syrie from behind her bedroom shutter.

Richard and Jenny simultaneously straightened. Family unity, thought Amanda wistfully.

'Let's play shark in the pool,' she said gaily. She leapt into the pool behind Emily and followed her thin energetic limbs under water. Emily screamed with excitement.

'Go way, go way,' she panted, her small face inches away from Amanda, who dived back under the water, moving languorously behind the child minnow. She liked this game, even after they had played it, at Emily's insistence, about twenty times. She liked Emily. She fervently hoped she was not using Emily to demonstrate her acceptability to Richard. That would be extremely bad taste.

Emily displayed a cat-like loyalty to Amanda now she had demonstrated pool skills. She sat at her feet, limbs folded inwards like a piece of origami a blue towel round her shoulders and a small pool of water under her.

'Come inside and get dry,' fussed Jenny, who tried to avoid getting wet when she was swimming.

'Mummy, I'm fine,' said Emily, pushing her chin into her chest.

'At least let's get you under a hairdryer, you'll get rat's tails,' said Jenny, lifting her daughter's head up with her fingertips.

Emily resisted.

'Amanda isn't drying her hair.'

Amanda looked straight ahead of her to avoid Emily's conspiratorial glance. She ran a hand through her own straight, wet hair.

'Maybe a hairdryer would get rid of the tangles,' she said. 'Pop stars don't have tangles do they?'

Emily wriggled delightedly.

'Britney wears her hair like this. At the front. Mine is long enough for that.'

'Oh, do let me see what it would look like,' said Amanda.

Emily jumped up. 'I'll show you. Will you come and watch if I have the hairdryer?'

'Why don't you get it all done properly and then come to show us?' suggested Amanda.

'OK. Come on, Mum, follow me.'

Amanda was surprised by the ease with which she engaged this child. She had always felt awkward in the company of colleagues' children. She knew the form: examining family snaps, screwing up her eyes to determine parental likeness, finding one attractive feature to comment on, but when children were brought physically into the office she could think of nothing to say to them. She felt she needed props – toys or sweets. She had always been depressed by the scene in *Mary Poppins* where the Banks children were shown the desiccated futility of the bank. And sad that they refused to invest their money in it, choosing to waste it on pigeons which were a health hazard and a public nuisance.

But now she saw there needn't be a secret language. She felt companionable. The swimming pool was the key that opened the lock to both the father and the daughter. The juxtaposition of the two should make her squeamish, but, God forgive her, it made her happy.

Richard got up from his chair and came and stood next to her. The back of his shoulders and neck had a radiation glow to them.

'Look at you, you're burnt,' exclaimed Amanda.

'Nonsense, it is a Sacha Distel tan,' he said turning his head awkwardly, like an old crane.

'It would hurt if I touched you,' said Amanda.

'No, it would definitely make it better. Please, nurse.'

'Who is Sacha Distel, Dad?' called Toby from the door.

Richard moved away from Amanda's sunbed.

'What, son? Who is Sacha Distel? Don't you know anything about French culture?'

'Only post-war,' said Toby, carrying a drink in his hand. He was almost as tall as Richard and dressed similarly in shorts and T-shirt, but his clothes hung differently on his slender frame and his face was more finely featured. The oak and the sapling, thought Amanda, in a glow of sentiment. Richard slapped an arm the size of a discus thrower round Toby's neck.

'Got a drink for me?'

Toby's torso shook with the impact and soda water spilt over his wrist.

'Careful, Dad. I'll go and fetch some. Amanda, what would you like?'

Amanda was a cautious drinker. Alcohol affected Derek's metabolism easily, so she was careful to keep pace with him. It was barely six p.m. now. She hesitated.

'What about a large G and T?' said Richard, lifting his thick, greying eyebrows. She was fascinated by the way his features moved from sternness to comedy. Even his square jaw acquired a jaunty wobble. His complexion was the colour of raw steak. She smiled at the sight of him.

'That would be lovely.'

'And Derek? What does he drink?' asked Toby.

Where was Derek? How had he moved without her noticing? She was tuned to rise whenever his limbs twitched.

'I'll go and see,' she said. 'He must have gone to lie down.'

'I'm here,' said Derek from behind her. 'I wasn't lying down, I went for a walk round the garden.'

He lowered himself onto a chair, arranging his weak legs in a straight line in front of him.

'Oh, darling, how did you manage? You could have fallen,' said Amanda sorrowfully.

'That chap helped me. I was fine. I'm not a total cripple,' said Derek, folding his arms over his chest in an unconscious imitation of Richard.

'Can I have a spritzer?' he asked Toby, smiling pleasantly. Amanda had become so used to studying another man's visage she had forgotten Derek's delicate lips and perfect teeth. He had a nice face, a really nice face. She sighed and wiggled her toes. It was flattering and alarming to have two men watching her. Her stomach curdled with anxiety, her heart pumped with desire. She shut her eyes and sighed again. If she lay quite still one or both might approach her and kiss her and, strangely, she did not mind which it was.

Then she felt something brush across her cheek. It was soft and ticklish. She opened her eyes and looked into Emily's bright little face.

'Are you asleep? Did you feel my hair? I tip-toed up to you. Are you surprised?'

Amanda put her hand on the child's warm, bony shoulder.

'I dreamt a cat walked over my face.'

Emily laughed.

'A cat? My hair isn't like fur. It is like Britney's.'

'It is. How did you get it into bunches? You know, your mother used to wear her hair like that when she was at school.'

'And did you wear your hair in bunches too?'

Amanda pictured herself at school, straight parting, tall, busty. No, she would not have worn bunches.

'I wasn't really the type,' she said.

'What type were you?' said Emily with interest. She was confident in her new friendship.

'Well, I worked hard. And swam and played hockey. I was head girl.'

'And do head girls not wear bunches?'

'Not really. They tend not to.'

Emily pulled fiercely at the toggles on her hair, her small teeth bared.

'I don't want them either, then.'

'Oh, Emily, what are you doing?' cried Jenny, appearing in

front of them brandishing a hairbrush. 'I went to so much effort. Look, we were going to be twins.'

Jenny too had acquired Britney bunches, which hung deflated over her forehead.

'You look silly, Mummy,' said Emily kindly. 'Take them off.'

Jenny swung her head defiantly.

'I like them. I'm going to keep them.'

Emily curled up alongside Amanda, entangling her thin legs with Amanda's heavy, adult calves.

'My mum is so embarrassing.'

Richard grabbed the hair-filled toggles from Emily's fist.

'I'm going to have Britney bunches,' he said arranging his thick forelock into two horns.

He hopped from one foot to another and thrust his hips forward.

'Skater boy,' he sang.

'Daaad, that's not Britney, that's Avril. Oh my God,' Emily wailed, pressing her face into Amanda's chest.

'Don't swear,' said Richard and Jenny together.

Once more Amanda felt pushed to the margins of the family. Her connections with father and daughter may be temporarily eclipsing, but parental bonds are strong.

'So, Jenny, your last day of being thirty-nine,' said Derek. He had laughter lines round his eyes, while the thicker lines across his forehead were the result of physical pain.

'Don't remind me,' tinkled Jenny. 'Goodbye youth. Yes, Toby, youth.'

Toby held his palms up in surrender.

'She's kept her figure all right,' said Richard. 'And not a grey hair in that head.'

Amanda nodded enthusiastically. Did Richard think women grew naturally blonder as they got older? That was the difference between the sexes. Women noticed and gave credit to the effortful process, while men saw only the final effect. They were less watchful, more generous. It was part of Richard's sweetness that he was proud of his wife, while simultaneously making advances to her best friend. He did not seem to register any contradiction.

Amanda's drink made her pleasantly woozy. These sexual urges occurred at inappropriate times, perhaps because there was no conventional outlet for them. They could not be accommodated in the domestic routines of the day. She was not going to enjoy the cosy, mechanical lights-out sex, which was the preserve of the married couple.

In compensation, she had had the best sex of her life in three minutes flat against the wall at the side of the house. She and Richard had been clearing the table, while Jenny and Daisy washed up inside. In the darkness, Richard had grabbed her wrist and she had stumbled after him in silence. She had been bruised by the weight of him slamming into her, and her back was sore and scratched from the rough stone. There had been no endearments, no vows, just a violent shared pulse. Then they had returned to stacking plates, light headed and dry mouthed from the aftershock.

The act was repeated in slow motion, her head crashing back onto the stone so that she felt her skull for blood. Then Richard stroked her cheek with contrasting tenderness. She kissed the hand gratefully.

'My wild girl,' whispered Derek. 'What were you dreaming of?'

The darkness was lifting outside, giving pale grey substance to the buildings and the bushes. Amanda shifted and straightened the bedclothes and pillows around her.

'It is so hot in here,' she murmured, patting Derek's hand and pushing it away from her.

'I know,' he said calmly. 'It'll be nice to get back, don't you think? To be a bit cooler.'

'Are you homesick?' she asked, staring at the ceiling.

'I suppose I am in a way. I like our life at home.'

She sensed his eyes fixed on her, wanting endorsement.

'I bet the plants need watering. There hasn't been any rain there, either,' she said.

'We can get some new plants. And we'll replace the sitting-room curtains. There are lots of ways we can make things nicer.'

Amanda felt a tear wind its way across her left temple. She squeezed Derek's hand and they lay still, companionably.

After a few minutes the silence was broken by raised voices down the corridor.

'Is that it? Napkins?'

Amanda and Derek turned their faces towards each other.

'Jenny?' whispered Derek.

'Her birthday present.'

There was a crash, a book or a lamp falling, and a low, reasoning voice drowned by a rising wail.

'Boring, bloody napkins! Well, thanks a lot.'

The door slammed and there was the sound of running footsteps followed by the emphatic banging of a heavier door. Jenny had taken off down the drive.

'Not *Breakfast at Tiffany's*, then?' said Derek.

Amanda pulled the cover over their heads.

'Battle stations! Hide,' she said, with muffled laughter.

At breakfast, Jenny appeared elaborately made-up and excessively dignified.

'Oh, really, you shouldn't have bothered,' she said, when Daisy and Toby presented her with a bunch of wilting flowers and a T-shirt that read 'Ready to Go'.

The croissants burnt while Jenny arranged each drooping stem in a huge vase, and then apologized while everybody chorused that it was not her fault.

Amanda thought that in the circumstances it would be tactless to present her with the tablecloth that matched the bloody boring napkins, so she squeezed Jenny's shoulder and told her that her gift would be to pay for the dinner. Jenny gave a tight, bright smile.

'Oh, don't even think about it. I'm much too old to care about birthdays.'

When Emily gravely handed over her card on which she had drawn Jenny and Richard, stick hands joined, outside a house painted in primary colours with a bright blue sky full of stars, Jenny hugged her daughter until she squealed for breath.

'Mummy, you'll break me. Stop!'

'Sorry, darling, it's just so nice of you to have gone to all that trouble.'

'That's not it, Mummy, that's just the card. Come with me.'

She led Jenny outside to show her an expertly made pot in rich aubergine, decorated with sapphire-coloured flowers.

Jenny carried it to the kitchen table with a luminously reproachful smile.

'That is the most beautiful birthday present I have ever received,' she breathed, with a sweeping glance that finally rested on Richard.

He shuffled miserably closer to take a look.

'Did you do that, Emily?'

'Yes, I did,' she said. 'I promise you. Ahmed started me off, but he said it was all my own work. If anyone asked, it was all my own work.'

Eight

Amanda thought that, since it was Jenny's birthday, it would be an unfriendly act to sleep with her husband. An absolute morality had to be adjusted to small acts of kindness. She was content to subjugate her needs so long as it was not for ever. She decided to take herself off for a long walk, secure in the knowledge that Richard would be aware of her absence and hopeful that he would miss her.

It was paradoxical that her affair had given her a taste for solitude. She was used to dividing her time methodically between work and Derek. An extra man made her seek some time for herself. She set off briskly without explanation down the drive then took a sharp turn into a scorched field which led to a pine forest and beyond that, the sea. The coastal path was vertiginous and Amanda quickly became parched. She sat down on a flat, jutting rock and looked down at the navy-blue water, dotted with white speed boats. She followed the progress of a small lizard on the edge of a stone. It was like grandmother's footsteps, the lizard moved only when she looked away. She debated whether the climb down would be worth it for a swim. The path was surrounded by large rocks which formed a frozen landslide. A sign said DANGER.

The coast stretched for miles, she could go to the nearest town and then walk back, but she was hot and thirsty and needed a pee. And she shouldn't leave Derek for that long. She picked at a blade of wild grass, which cut her index finger. Discomfort was as worthy of consideration as greater peril. The dislodged rocks, the currents of the sea, the lashing sun and the route home were of less concern to her than her lightly throbbing hand. She got up and made her way back, considering the strange trio that awaited her: her husband, her friend, her lover.

She remembered grave discussions with Jenny about whom they would marry. They must have been twelve at the time. There had never been a question of multiples. One man, one life. The hardest thing about adulthood was choice.

The path forked several times and she was fearful of taking a wrong turn. The sun was pounding down on her head, and a canal of sweat ran down her back making her shirt and shorts stick to her like clingfilm. You would not want to get lost in this heat. Fortunately, Amanda had made a successful career out of noticing details – a mark on a tree, a collapsing fence, a field full of sunflowers – and she found her way back just as her throat was beginning to swell with dryness.

*

The group had hardly moved during these lost hours, assembling in their habitual places by the pool with amiable irritability.

Richard had taken Emily's lilo and was half sinking it with his weight. An arm and leg were submerged and his large red belly formed a sandbank above the water. He wriggled and fell off. Jenny was sunbathing in the deckchair, her face barely visible under a large hat and sunglasses, her hands clenched on the wooden sides as if she were on the deck of a ship entering choppy waters. Daisy and Toby were playing Scrabble with Derek. Gerry was snoring in a chair in the shade, with a regular chorus of wheezes and grunts. Syrie was making a flower chain, digging her long nails viciously into the stalks.

'God,' she wailed after a seismic shudder from Gerry's chair. 'Aren't men awful away from the office? Remove the suit and the desk and they all turn into granddads.'

Richard shook water from each ear and grinned at her.

'Are you finding the pace a bit slow here, Syrie?'

'Tell me about it.' She grimaced. 'I think holidays are just too long. It is unnatural to go from 24/7 to, like, nothing. We should be more like America. They don't have this holiday culture, not at all.'

Jenny raised her head, like a bird. The conversation had at last turned to her specialist subject.

'But what are they working for in America?' she asked.

'Good question,' chuckled Richard.

Jenny propped herself up on her elbows. Praise from her husband! Maybe her forties weren't going to be so bad.

'You are being facetious, right?' said Syrie. 'I mean anyone with a work ethic doesn't see it as a means to anything. It's the only way to live. Keeps the blood flowing. Can you imagine what it is like not to work? To be like ... like that lizard on the rock over there. Just awful.'

Jenny retreated under her hat. Is that how she seemed to everyone? Like a lizard. She pressed her long oval nails into her hands and gulped.

'I'm not sure I want work to be the biggest thing in my life,' said Daisy, looking up from her Scrabble letters. 'You know, it's not so important. My dad ... Gerry used to say that no one looks back on their life and wishes they had spent more time in the office.'

Syrie tipped back her head theatrically.

'Please don't say Gerry used that old cliché. What was that from – a Christmas cracker? A constituency rubber-chicken dinner?'

Daisy flushed and shuffled her position clockwise away from Syrie.

As she moved Toby noticed a small butterfly tattooed at the base of her spine. He decided not to draw attention to it in case her father didn't know, and got stressed. But he couldn't quite get it or its canvas of flesh out of his mind.

Everyone fell quiet, excused by the heat from defending

Daisy. Heavens, this holiday was becoming anthropological, thought Derek, a series of territorial disputes and mating calls.

'Oh look, here's Amanda,' said Richard, displacing a layer of water as he lifted his arm in welcome. 'How did you manage to sneak away?'

Amanda got a drink and sat down at the shady side of the pool near Derek and stretched out her legs. If only she could wave everyone else away so Richard could slide into her. Sex was her only interest now, she thought.

'I walked down to the sea. It was beautiful,' she said dreamily.

'Why don't you go for a walk, Syrie?' said Jenny unpleasantly. 'It would do you good.'

'Yeah, well,' said Syrie. 'I guess I should wait to see how Gerry is. He might get tetchy if I'm missing. First you're a lover, then you're a nurse, eh?'

'Or the other way round,' murmured Derek.

Amanda looked at him sharply. He looked back at her, his eyes cloudy. Nobody else seemed to have heard. Daisy moved her plastic squares nimbly into a new formation.

'Lots of lovely consonants,' she said in her sweet, faux south London voice.

'What have you got?' asked Derek.

'I'm not showing you,' she said. 'I have to see if I can place it.'

'Can I see what you've got?' asked Amanda gaily.

Daisy moved towards her on her knees, shielding her plastic panel with her hand. The word was 'betrays'.

'Ah, yes, good,' said Amanda faintly.

'Yeah, but it doesn't fit,' said Daisy, wrinkling her nose. 'It's too long to go downwards. So annoying, I could have picked up a double and a treble.'

'I think I'm going inside to get ready for dinner,' announced Jenny. 'Last chance to look my best.'

'Hey, life doesn't end at forty,' said Syrie. 'Maybe thirty . . .'

'What is it exactly that women do for two hours?' said Richard, paddling jauntily across the pool on his lilo.

'Oh, you know, darling, change their underpants,' Jenny shot back.

'Hey,' he said, throwing a rubber ball at her.

That was the result of having a mistress, thought Amanda sadly. They made husbands good-natured towards their wives.

She felt a light, damp pair of arms around her neck.

'Can we play the shark game?' asked Emily.

Amanda stroked the glistening blonde hairs on Emily's forearm, then reached behind her to gather up the dainty torso, really not much more than a spine and a bony bottom. As she jumped in the pool with Emily on her back, she thought, I would sacrifice my life for this girl. That was the contract between an adult and a child, whatever the relationship.

*

The Villa

They parked the cars at the bottom of the hill and climbed up the path to the village. The women were all wearing black: Jenny, a cocktail dress; Syrie, a jumpsuit; Amanda in a smart, anonymous boxy suit that she kept for board meetings; Daisy, a long stretchy skirt and black T-shirt. She was the fleshiest: not yet conditioned to life on a gym treadmill.

Gerry and Richard were in jacket and tie; Derek, a cream linen suit, which had become too big for him; Toby, arrestingly handsome, in a blue shirt and jeans. He unfolded the wheel-chair from the boot and pushed Derek up the winding road, with humorous stops and starts as if entertaining a toddler. Derek, who was usually treated with pity disguised as respect, giggled delightedly.

Emily had stayed behind with Jessica Arnout. Although she had protested – offering to be on her best behaviour, doubting her parents' love for her, pleading with Amanda and finally shutting herself in her room, where she sobbed at intervals between listening for reactions – Emily had a child's awareness of her ultimate impotence. She had finally resorted to looking tragic as she watched the party leave, a ghostly face at the window, until her father made faces at her and she had to frown hard to stop herself laughing. When Jenny went back to retrieve her forgotten handbag, she reported that Emily was playing hangman with Madame Arnout by the pool and had not even turned round as she said goodnight.

Amanda had trained herself not to wish for children. She

had a prepared defence, which was that children were all right when they belonged to somebody else. She was not much interested in her legacy, looking forward in a way to having her life tidied up, finished and dated. She knew there was always going to be the potential for morbidity in her relationship with Derek: a grim, resigned decline; an elongated quiet suffering. When she thought of the two of them, just the two of them, eking out their lives, her heart sometimes sank like a rock.

She skipped ahead to join Richard, Jenny and Daisy. Particularly Richard.

'You remind me of Emily, dancing about like that,' he said. His good mood had lasted for days. Amanda felt a warm contentment at having pleased the boss.

'It isn't the same without Emily,' she replied, although truthfully it was a difference for the better. Children had to be the centre of attention and for now she did not want Richard distracted. She basked in his pleasure and desire. She walked rather too close to him, their bodies bumping as they turned a corner. Jenny slipped back with Daisy; Syrie walked a few paces behind them humming tunelessly to herself, Gerry shuffled behind her looking hopelessly out of sorts.

'You look beautiful,' whispered Richard, extending an arm to guide Amanda out of the way of a car. Amanda widened her eyes at him and parted her lips. Particles of energy bounced back and forth between them. I will never be weary with this man, she thought to herself. She glanced back at

Jenny whose expression was blank. Amanda liked Jenny and did not wish to inflict pain, but this was probably her last chance of happiness before the grave and happiness usually came at another person's expense. That was a fact of life. It was selfish to claim Richard but it was cowardly not to.

'I'm looking forward to this,' she said heartily.

The road wound into the heart of the fortress village. The restaurant was built in heavy stone. It was small and serious. Diners sniffed at their wine and talked in low murmurs. At the front was a balcony with cinematic views over smaller hills and down to the dark sea. There was a light breeze, which threatened to become a wind. The candles on the large oblong table, marked reserved, flickered uncertainly. Jenny bustled to the front.

'This is ours. Now, seating. Let's mix up sexes and ages. I'll start here with Gerry and Toby on either side. Then . . . um . . . Derek, you plump yourself here, then you have a bit of room behind you. Let's put Syrie next to you. Richard you sit next to Daisy. So, that leaves Amanda.'

'Why doesn't Amanda sit on one side of me and Daisy the other?' suggested Richard helpfully.

Jenny frowned. 'That means putting Daisy next to Syrie. That isn't going to work.'

'Why not?' asked Syrie. 'Don't women have anything to say to each other? Come on, surely we can discuss cross stitch or something.'

Jenny stuck out her bottom lip.

'Actually, I was thinking of Daisy. You know . . .'

'It's OK,' said Daisy with a pained smile. 'I'll sit next to Syrie.'

Syrie gave a cross gasp and sat down, winding her pashmina round her chair.

'We'll probably have to go inside anyway once the mistral gets going.'

'Let's order some wine,' said Richard, winking at Amanda.

Amanda sat down dutifully, her heart skipping with triumph. She felt Richard's hand grapple with her thigh beneath the tablecloth. She admired his risk-taking.

'Mmm, now what shall I have?' she said, studying her menu.

'Apart from me,' whispered Richard, his sun-crisped eyelids closing in a wink.

It took fifteen minutes to arrive at a consensus and to order in French. Jenny tried to establish a relationship with the phlegmatic-looking waitress.

'My birthday.' She nodded, widening her eyes and simulating blowing out the candle. It went out and the waitress disappeared to find matches.

'One of us must be able to speak decent French!' she said gaily. 'Come on, Gerry. You are the expert on foreign affairs.'

Gerry gave an anxious nod. He was sweating profusely, although the temperature had dropped with the breeze.

'Do you want me to do the ordering?' asked Syrie dryly.

'Oh, I think it is nice to leave that to the men, don't you?' replied Jenny firmly.

She swivelled towards Gerry in an upright Barbie-doll gesture and rubbed her pastel-pink lips together.

'Now, Gerry, would you tell the waitress that I will start with the artichoke, followed by . . . let me see . . . oh, why not as it's my birthday? I'll have the millions of calories duck and—'

There was a crash beside her as Gerry's head hit the table.

Nine

Daisy sat alone in the darkness by the pool. She had wanted to stay at the hospital – he was her dad – but the grown-ups had decided it was better for everyone to come back to the villa and snatch a few hours' sleep. Like, their decisions had been great so far. If only her mum were here, if only everything could be as it used to be. Daisy stifled a sob and clenched her hands together. She had been dead scared this evening. When her dad collapsed like that his face had looked so weird and there had been dribble coming out of his mouth. And it had seemed to take place in slow motion: the wine tipping over the table, the plate of olives scattering. God, and Jenny picking up the olives as if it mattered. People shouting and everyone running about. And then the blue light of the ambulance outside, the French guys – the paramedics in their uniforms. Watching her dad being lifted onto a stretcher. She could hear her own voice in the babble, 'Dad, are you OK? Dad?' It was so awful and, you know, it was embarrassing too. She hadn't known what to do. Then Richard had pushed her into the ambulance and got in beside her, squashing against her. She didn't really know Richard or Jenny, they were like strangers; she'd wanted her mum. But the worst thing was watching Syrie cradle her dad's head like it was her tragedy. She had started all of this. Daisy shivered. That was mean; it was nobody's fault, it was just lives getting out of control.

Jenny had taken Daisy's hand and whispered, 'Do you want to hold him? Go on, he's your father.' Daisy didn't want to cause any trouble, but she had leant forward and stroked a place on his elbow which was free of wires. She was too terrified to bawl. She could feel her dad's flesh, but not her own numb fingers. His arm moved away from her in a reflex reaction. Pain is lonely, fear is lonely. He wasn't thinking of his daughter. Daisy had cleared her throat to stop herself crying. She had looked at the ambulance men to see how seriously they were taking this. One of them winked at her. Maybe it would be OK. She thought it might be worse that her father was so ill in a foreign country, but she hoped medicine had no frontiers.

Then the ambulance had raced through the gates of a big modern building and there had been staff to meet them.

Someone had asked who Gerry's next of kin was and Richard had hesitated. He pointed at Daisy and then at Syrie. Like hell she was. Daisy thought Syrie had probably gone off the idea of being a next of kin. She must have believed she was with this big powerful guy but the next moment she was saddled with a loser. That's why you had to marry young, so you rode the wave better. Or not marry at all. It was pretty hypocritical to take all those vows and then just dump the dude at the first opportunity.

Daisy hit a mosquito buzzing about on her upper arm. She was going to look like a measles case by the morning, but who cared? Who cared about Daisy? Like all those pieces in newspapers by middle-aged journalists on how children changed everything – different priorities, unconditional love, blah blah – making a living out of your children more like. Trying to look like you are a nice person, when it only takes one extra marital shag and you totally lose it. Oh God, and now her father might die and it was probably her fault. If only she had done her homework better and not pissed him off with wanting lifts all the time maybe he would have been happier at home. Maybe her mum wouldn't have got so stressed. Dear God, please let Dad live.

Daisy looked up at the vast sky and those faraway stars. It was a dark indifferent world. It couldn't give a shit. She was just some stupid girl.

Her body released another shuddering sob. This was a big deal; welcome to adulthood Daisy. Her dad would not be waiting up for her in his dressing gown; he would not be taking her on a tour of the House of Commons and lunch at Pizza Express; he would not be making terrible jokes to her teachers and her boyfriends; he would not be picking her up from late-night parties – he would be a different person or nobody, buried, gone. Her dad. And really she would prefer it if he were snorting cocaine at Brixton Academy or making a total arse of himself with Syrie. Please God, just keep him alive.

Daisy folded herself into a foetal position on the chair. Finally, after what could have been hours or minutes, a figure approached. Toby hugged Daisy's shivering body and helped her into the house. Daisy had so wanted someone to come and find her and was so relieved it was Toby. Everyone needed a bit of kindness – she most of all.

Daisy didn't know how long she slept that night. It was like being on a plane. Nodding off and then starting awake, always alert – in case. She even had a strange body breathing close to her. Toby had lain down across the bottom of her bed. It was so sweet of him, though it meant she couldn't move her feet. She was so scared for her dad, somewhere else in his own strange bed with lights and monitors and people speaking in a different language. She should have insisted that she slept in a chair in his room or something, but she hadn't known how to ask and nobody had asked her what she wanted. And in a way, that was a relief. The intimacy would have been so weird. Like seeing him with his pyjamas flapping open, and what if he wet himself or something? Not that she couldn't have coped, she wasn't a total bitch. But it would have scared her. There were some things you did not want to associate with your parents. Like farting or sex. Or illness. Parents look after children. And that's it. It is so gross, so terrifying for it to be the other way round.

Anyway, she had travelled back in the car, so cold. Jenny had tried to make conversation about holidays or something. When they arrived back at the villa, Amanda had offered to make everyone a cup of tea. Daisy had felt safer in company, but Jenny was yawning badly and finally people dispersed. That was when Daisy had gone to sit outside. She had bidden goodnight to everyone first, and told Jenny she was sorry that her birthday party had been spoilt.

The phone rang at about 3 a.m. – Daisy's heart was thumping like a DJ's sound system. She lurched out of bed and tried to work out where the sound was coming from. When she got to the phone in the kitchen, Richard was already there in a nightshirt thing. He handed the phone to Daisy. 'It's your mum.'

Daisy felt home reaching her in warm waves down the phone. She gabbled a bit, wanting to tell her mother everything, but knowing she also had a responsibility to shield her. She didn't mention Syrie by name and didn't go on about all the sex and stuff. Her eyes filled with tears when her mother asked her if she had taken any drugs. In the end that was what really mattered to mothers.

'I love you, Mum. I guess I'll be home soon.' Her voice echoed round the dim room. She was shivering. 'See you soon, Mum.'

She replaced the receiver, scurried back to bed and drew the sheets over her face. Make the world normal and safe again, make this all be over, she thought.

Everyone's wide-awake faces appeared at breakfast, looking as if they had all come out of a wind tunnel. They all behaved with unnatural calm. Amanda sat next to Daisy and started asking her about university courses. She had lost all her twitchiness. When Daisy had been playing Scrabble with Derek and had shown Amanda the word 'betrays', Amanda had looked freaked out; she had jumped about six miles. But now she was very neat and matter of fact. She was probably used to dealing with heart attacks in the office. Hyperventilating businessmen, that kind of thing. They must all have really high blood pressure, and totally screwed-up digestive systems and sleeping patterns as a result of flying to all those different meetings. Probably BUPA nipped a lot of heart trouble in the bud, but what if the businessmen missed their appointments because they were playing golf or something? Or what if they had heart attacks *while* playing golf? In Portugal. Amanda must have worked out the options. Anyway, she was not fazed by Gerry's sex-induced collapse. Not at all.

'This is just the body issuing a warning,' said Amanda. She was wearing a dark dress, a little funereal for Daisy's mood, but she thought it suited her. She had a good figure; she was skinnier than Daisy. That was something to look forward to, she supposed, the flesh getting thinner. She looked down at her big fat boobs under her T-shirt. Yuk, really. Not that it mattered right now.

'But what if there's permanent damage?' said Daisy.

'Oh, that would be very unlucky. It probably means your father will have to slow down a bit, take more care. But there are so many pills that can regulate your heart. And the health system in France is terribly good. Those doctors last night really knew what they were doing.'

Daisy felt the humming in her ears subside. She lapped up Amanda's words. She of all people would know about the body's limits.

'Was it hard for you when Derek was diagnosed?' she asked shyly. She brushed away the croissant crumbs stuck to her face. She should have finished her mouthful properly before speaking.

Amanda gave a rueful smile.

'Not as hard as it was for Derek. But you know, you have

to take what life throws at you and not run away from it. You have to be a stronger person.'

Daisy liked that idea. She wanted to write it down. When someone said something profound – a character in a book or in real life – she stored it up. She wanted a moral code to live by. Some of the quotations in her exercise book sucked when she looked back at them – she was really embarrassed by the stuff from Disney cartoons and pop songs – she had learned 'Wear Sunscreen' by heart when it was really pretty stupid, but she wanted to learn. Derek had given her a philosophy book, which was really interesting. She wanted to learn wisdom from the unfortunate. Oh, and from old people. Especially in homes. She really liked hearing about the war and stuff, and how people coped with rationing. Although, sometimes the people in homes just stared into space and said nothing. She didn't know what she could learn from that. Maybe the wisdom of silence or something. All those TV presenters and the casts of reality shows should learn about silence. Although you needed to say something as well, because silence wasn't very good TV.

Richard came outside with his cup of coffee.

'Who wants to come to the hospital?' he said in a friendly way, as if he were proposing a picnic. Daisy said, yeah, and brushed the rest of the crumbs from her T-shirt. She hoped Richard hadn't heard her talking to her mum, sounding like a total child. She was an adult, but she felt more like Emily; she just wanted to curl up and howl. If she did that, she reckoned it would be with Amanda. Even though Amanda didn't have any children of her own, she had the best vibes. Daisy felt she could trust her. She stood up, almost losing her balance as she did so. There was something gravity-defying about fear, she felt weird and weightless. Well, a bit on the chubby side to be weightless. When would life start to feel normal again? She just wanted her dad to be well, only that. And to be home. And not to cry in front of these people.

'Good luck,' said Amanda, stretching out her hand. 'Derek and I are going to head off today, but I'll phone you of course, and we will be thinking of you.'

Richard made a funny clicking noise and stared at Amanda. Maybe he was scared of having to cope alone. She was way more easy-going than Jenny, that was for sure. Richard seemed more natural, more himself with Amanda. Daisy hoped he wasn't going to have heart trouble as well. She should have done a first-aid course before agreeing to this holiday. She had thought adults didn't start conking out until they retired.

Amanda got up briskly and walked back indoors. Daisy could have sworn she saw tears in her eyes. It was a pretty emotional time for everyone. As she walked with Jenny to Richard's car at the front of the house Daisy heard Amanda and Derek talking in their bedroom. She wasn't listening; it was just that their bedroom window was always open – a burglar could have walked right in. Derek sounded pretty agitated.

'Darling, we don't have to do this. I know what you're thinking – that one invalid is enough on this holiday. But, good Lord, Gerry and I might keep each other company. You don't have to be ward sister, I promise.'

'That's not it, Derek, don't be silly,' said Amanda, sounding muffled. Maybe she was bending down packing, but she might have been crying a bit. 'We're just better off on our own, back home. I don't think we mix very well.'

'You mix very well, darling,' said Derek, his voice cracking. 'I'm the one holding you back. If it weren't for me . . .'

'Oh, for God's sake,' said Amanda, clearly, having moved closer to the window. 'Don't play for sympathy. I am with you because you are clever and sweet and we agreed for better or for worse. I am the problem here, not you. I am spoiling our happiness because . . . because . . . I don't think holidays agree with me, that's all. Now give me your suitcase.'

Daisy felt her stomach clang even lower. As if it weren't bad enough that her dad was gravely ill, now Amanda had turned her back on her. She didn't like the crowd here, obviously, and that included Daisy. Doubly rejected Daisy. Her face twisted in misery but when she turned round, she saw Richard with genuine, honest-to-God tears in his eyes. This was really freaky – an adult crying because a guest wasn't enjoying her holiday? His lip was turned right down like a fat kid's, then he rubbed his hands up and down his face.

'Sorry, I just forgot something inside,' muttered Daisy.

She went to her room and sat there until it was safe – from what? Well, from adults crying for a start. She heard Amanda dragging cases along the corridor, sounding, you know, quite jaunty. Then a car's engine. Was it them or Richard? She rubbed her arms, still feeling disconnected from her physical self. It was either trauma or she was having a stroke too; she wouldn't put it beyond this place. It was, like, cursed.

Daisy rubbed the goose pimples on her arms a bit harder, then started to cast around for her stuff, chapstick for her lips, magazines, some euros – she wondered what to do about money, she had been relying on her dad for the money to get home and for going out – should she mention this to Jenny?

There was a faint knock on her door, which was open. It was Syrie.

'OK if I come in?' she asked. She had junked her femme fatale breakfast costumes and was wearing a baggy old T-shirt and tracksuit bottoms. She looked really young. 'Are you going to the hospital?' she asked, nervously, as if Daisy might be planning a shopping expedition.

'Yes, just leaving,' said Daisy, pushing her thin wad of notes into her jeans.

'OK with you if I come too?' asked Syrie, looking at the ceiling.

Aha, so the relationship dynamics were changing. Daisy was at the centre; Daisy would pick up the pieces. She wanted to be haughty but she didn't know how, and she suddenly felt surprisingly affectionate towards Syrie. Daisy wanted to look after her dad, but she probably wouldn't want to look after someone else's dad, or sleep with them for that matter. Syrie had a bum deal, that was for sure.

As she passed her in the doorway, Daisy held out her hand. It was a daft gesture, midway between nothing and a hug. Syrie took her hand and gave it a quick shake. Then they both walked silently out of the house to the waiting car.

Gerry was sitting up in his bed when they got there. He looked about a hundred, his face and hair all the wrong colour, like Tony Curtis or somebody. And he was wearing a smock. You had to put your ear really close to hear him speak; Daisy hadn't been that physically near to him for a long time. But Daisy wasn't scared, she was glad because it could have been worse. In her dream, he had looked like the mummy in the film with the really pretty actress. Her heart pumped with dread and relief. Syrie spoke to the doctor, very fast and fluently. It was pretty impressive. Then she took Daisy's hand across the bed, but this time she didn't shake it, she just stroked it in a very kind way.

'It was only a mild heart attack,' she said, her enlarged pupils making her eyes quite black. 'They'll keep him here for a few days, but they expect him to make a full recovery.' Her lips twitched ironically. 'For his age.'

Daisy nodded. 'That's good.' She looked at her father. 'That's good, Dad. That's good news.'

Then she turned her head away from him.

'I'm sure Mum will help. Mum and I can nurse him, you know.'

Syrie's shoulders deflated.

'Let's see how it goes, shall we?'

Daisy came out of the hospital into a wall of heat, having promised to return again in the afternoon. The holiday now had a grim purpose, replacing one routine with another. She felt grave and adult. Syrie put on her sunglasses and offered Daisy a cigarette. There were quite a few relatives outside, passing the time, smoking. Was it because they were French that there was a vaguely social atmosphere?

'You were great with the doctor,' said Daisy, pressing her fingers to her cigarette, which was already rather squashed and damp-looking. She wasn't a very stylish smoker. Syrie tilted her chin and blew determined puffs of smoke to the sky. She had this really neat little embroidered bag. She wasn't a bad person. If there were a lesson to all this, it was that people weren't nasty, just mucked up. Daisy kept the thought running, to put in her notebook later on.

She cocked her head at the animated smokers.

'What's making them so cheerful?' she asked companionably.

Syrie took a long drag.

'It's the local murder,' she said. 'Some Belgian student. Stabbed with a full set of kitchen knives! They're saying that extra police have been drafted in. It was in the paper. They're probably pleased because it was a tourist. You know, it would be a dull summer without the grisly murder of a tourist.'

Daisy laughed. She liked Syrie's worldliness. Her dad probably found it a relief from her mother's conventional anxieties. No sooner had she registered this disloyal thought than she felt the tug of homesickness. Her father's pleasure would always be balanced by her mother's misery, that was the awful seesaw of married life. She sighed with the weight of it.

A car horn beeped. Jenny was leaning out of the window, her mouth moving frantically beneath her sun visor.

'OK, girl,' said Syrie, stubbing out her cigarette beneath her open-toed sandal. 'I think the happily marrieds want to leave. They might lose their place by the pool.'

Daisy's cigarette had gone out anyway. It was a little bit bitchy of Syrie, but that was OK – if you looked like Syrie.

When they got back, Toby and Emily were laying the table.

'Is Gerry coming back from hospital? Shall I lay him a place anyway?' asked Emily, cutlery in hand, hip to one side, like her mum. She was a sweet kid, her eyes as big as plates.

'Just the five of us,' said Jenny, scooping up cutlery like a card trick.

'Hang on, what about Amanda and Derek?' said Emily, following her mother on her destructive course. 'Are they in hospital too?'

Toby took her hand.

'They went home, Em, that's why they had all that luggage.'

'But what about my swimming lessons?' Emily's mouth trembled.

'I'll swim with you,' said Daisy.

'But you don't know the shark game,' wailed Emily.

'I'll be a shark. Or a dolphin. They're kinder. We have to be kind to each other.'

'Amanda left a note for you, Daisy,' said Toby, pulling an envelope from his jeans' pocket.

It was pretty thick. Daisy hoped it wasn't an epistle. She hardly knew Amanda, but then she hardly knew anyone here, except Toby. It was like being on an exchange. She felt far away from home. Far away from her life.

She walked towards the pool. She didn't want people watching her, just in case she cried. The envelope contained a thick wad of euro notes, maybe a hundred pounds' worth. She hadn't mentioned that she was worried about money, had she? That was the difference with adults. They just *knew* things. The accompanying letter was only a page long.

Dear Daisy,

Here is something to tide you over. A little financial security is reassuring, I always think, especially when the rest of life seems uncertain. I am sure Gerry will be fine and I want you to be OK too. None of this is your responsibility. You have a good nature, but remember, you have the rest of your life ahead of you and you deserve to be happy. I want you to think of yourself. There's time enough to think of other people. Be free!

With very best wishes

Amanda

Daisy put away the letter. Well, yeah, of course she had her life ahead of her. So she had plenty of time to look after her poor old dad. She thought it odd of Amanda to write this because she obviously found it rewarding taking care of Derek.

He was such a nice guy and everything. She was sorry he hadn't stayed on because he was easy to talk to. It was sweet the way he got worked up about cycling. She would send him a postcard. It was the least she could do with all Amanda's money.

Daisy didn't feel much like eating, but she took Amanda's words to heart about living her own life and stuff, so she took the last bit of tomato and had seconds of Parma ham. She resolved to edit out what she ate from her notebooks because it wouldn't be very interesting in a book of wisdom, although it might be useful for future generations of schoolchildren should they ever come to study her book. Daisy had been interested in what the Romans ate.

Richard and Jenny suggested returning to the hospital in the early evening rather than in the afternoon, when it wasn't so hot. They could lie by the pool until then. Daisy didn't feel much like reading; it seemed disloyal to think about fictional characters when there was a real drama going on. She didn't feel like sitting down either. She wanted to keep moving.

'I think I'll go for a walk,' she announced tentatively.

Toby offered to come with her. Daisy partly wanted that. But there was the problem that she fancied Toby and it was wrong to be thinking about that right now. She had only realized it properly after last night when he had lain on her bed. He was great as a friend and it was nice sleeping with someone without actually, you know, sleeping with them. But let's face it, sex beats friendship. Toby was a dude, she could imagine . . . well, not at the moment, of course, that would be trashy and she was all tied up inside, but later, if it worked out, if God let her dad be OK and everything felt real again. It would be something to look forward to, starting a relationship with Toby. He seemed to like her. He had stared at her tattoo. She was glad Toby had noticed it and not her dad. But then, she had deliberately let her T-shirt ride up. Even before she had admitted to herself that she fancied Toby she had been trying to get her hair right and putting on lip gloss and stuff; she was more self-conscious than felt right for a chill-out holiday. That's how she knew, subconsciously, kind of in a Freudian way, that there was something going on between them.

On the other hand, Toby was pretty nice to everyone. Daisy hoped he would like her just because he could. They were both free, so why not hook up? Once Gerry was out of hospital.

'I feel like being alone,' she said in a small voice. The words just came out, whether or not she meant them. Everyone looked at her with those soft, understanding expressions.

'Take a bottle of water,' said Jenny. 'And don't go too far.'

'Shall I get you a map, show you where we are?' said Richard.

'I'll be OK,' said Daisy. 'I'll go the way Amanda went, towards the sea.'

'That's quite a long way,' said Jenny doubtfully.

'I won't go all the way. I'll be fine,' said Daisy, feeling tearful.

She gave a big wave and set off down the drive, turning into the first field. The blue and yellow flowers brushed against her legs below her shorts; the dust from the ground coated her ankles. It was a steep slope, so she walked at an angle. The scent of the pine trees could almost be bottled. Nature was a caressing, parental force, she thought. That could go into her notebook. It was strange being all alone; you would have thought someone would be walking a dog, or hiking. But then there was so much more space in France.

The way ahead was hazy with heat, and bobbles of sweat formed on her face. If this were school cross-country she would sing a pop song in her head, like 'Sugababes', but her spirits were too fretful. She had to think about the future. She could take a year out if her dad needed her, she was sure the universities would understand. Maybe she should phone her tutor when she got back. She both wanted the school to know and she didn't. Maybe she should wait for her A level results first. If they weren't good, she could definitely look after her dad and resit. If they were good . . . well, her mum could make the decision for her. She could always go home for weekends. And if she met someone, well, it could be every other weekend.

Daisy reached the wood. She stopped and took a swig of water. She could turn back now, but she hadn't resolved anything yet. This was to be a momentous walk; this would decide her future.

There was a grotesque screech nearby and something tore out of the bushes. Daisy screamed too as it hit her arm. The sound bounced across the top of the trees in an acoustic cacophony. It was a bird. It was just a bird. Daisy crouched down in the scorched bracken. Her breathing was ragged, like someone being strangled. Like her dad's had been before the paramedics fitted his oxygen mask. It was just a bird, but Daisy was so fearful.

'Steady, steady,' she said to herself. This was the country-side, there was no danger here. Stupid girl, she could not turn back now. She would walk all the way to the sea to show herself there was nothing to fear. The darkness was inside not outside. She strode along the little-trodden path, pushing aside stalks and brambles. She could no longer see the route behind her.

Daisy started to hum to herself. It came out as high pitched as an insect voice. She began again, lower. Her throat was dry as sand, but her heartbeat was slower. She took another swig of water. It was pretty here, she should appreciate it. She knew it was important to take pleasure in nature. This thought had already been underlined in her notebook. She could see the edge of the cliff and the calm cobalt-coloured sea. She would sit on the grass for a while and then head back. Perhaps there was no need to sit. Her thoughts were starting to repeat themselves and she did not want to be late for the hospital.

At the cliff edge, there was a narrow path which zigzagged down to an empty pebble beach below. A sign said DANGER. The path would be manageable if you hung onto the jutting branches on either side. There must have been a landslide of rocks long ago, but now the boulders were lodged on the cliff face. Daisy remembered that Amanda had mentioned a path to a beach. Perhaps Amanda too had been drawn to physical challenge in order to conquer an unquiet mind. She looked back uncertainly. At the edge of the wood something moved. That wasn't a bird, it was a person. Daisy stared at the figure, but it did not move, it did not walk on. Someone was hiding behind the tree. She waited. The man looked at her from the middle distance then turned his back. But he did not walk away. Daisy thought of the people outside the hospital and of the newspaper stories. Was this her fate?

Why hadn't she let Toby come with her? She didn't even have her phone. She looked sadly at the water bottle. It wasn't much of a weapon. The man remained motionless. Either their names would be connected catastrophically or they wouldn't. He might just walk away. Why shouldn't he? The only link between them at this moment was Daisy's unhappy imagination. She took a few steps towards him. He moved behind the tree. He was waiting for her. This man was here because of her. Daisy knew this to be true.

With sobbing breaths she turned back and slid down the path. She held onto a branch, which cracked so that she tumbled onto a rock below. A shower of stones scattered above and below her. The path was vertiginous and she scrambled on hands and feet. Daisy hugged a rock which immediately wobbled and moved like a rotten tooth. It hit another rock and then another like a game of skittles. A landslide had started.

Above the ghastly rumble of falling debris a man shouted, 'Daisy, jump, jump.'

Daisy looked up through dusty tears. Ahmed was waving at her from the top of the cliff.

'I can't.' She wept hopelessly, her limbs stiff with terror. 'I'm going to die. Help me!'

'You must jump. Run, jump,' shrieked Ahmed.

Daisy shook her head. She curled up as rocks bounced past her. The sea was forty metres away, she would die whatever happened. She would die in France. She would never know how her life might have turned out.

'Help me. Oh please help me,' she sobbed.

Ahmed was climbing down the cliff but the path had disappeared in collapsing rubble. He was perhaps twenty metres away. The cliff jutted above the concave inlet of the beach. Ahmed looked down from his ledge above her.

'If I jump, you jump,' he yelled.

Daisy crawled to the edge of her ledge.

'Look at me, look at me,' he said. Then he put his arms by his sides and ran off his ledge into the air, his legs jogging over her head, down, down, until he hit the water below. It looked both comic and terrifying.

Daisy did not wait. She ran from her ledge, treading the air, parachuting down until she felt the slap of the sea, sinking lower and lower, then beginning to rise again. She was soggy with water, it ran through her nostrils, ears and eyes. It felt as if she had been water skiing for ever – painful, but exhilarating – in other words, she was alive. Ahmed's head was bobbing only five metres or so away. He shook his head and raised an arm above him.

'OK Daisy? OK?'

Daisy laughed. She loved this feeling of survival, terror and happiness.

'Swim with me,' said Ahmed. She moved her bruised arms in breaststroke, swimming away from the collapsed beach, following the contours of the land from a safe distance. She could hear the sound of boat engines in the distance and even the shouts of swimmers. People were converging towards the drama. The process of emergency rescue was underway. A helicopter was humming overhead and three speed boats headed towards them, two with French flags.

As the drama became the centre of public attention, Daisy felt sobs pushing up from her chest.

'Oh, oh, oh,' she said.

Ahmed bobbed closer to her, supporting her arm. She gulped water and tears.

'What were you doing, Ahmed? Why were you following me?'

He shook his head, his eyes glowing amber.

'Help,' shouted Daisy. 'Help me.'

The boat engines chugged and then stopped. Two men in uniform – Police? Lifeguards? – threw an anchor overboard, then reached over the side of the boat and hauled Daisy up. Her shorts billowed with water, her T-shirt was rolled up over her shoulders as if she had been in a spin cycle. Her hearing was muffled by the water in her ears and her head felt compressed and bruised. She was wrapped in blankets, and asked a series of questions she could not translate. She used a few of the diving signs she remembered and feebly thanked everyone for their trouble. As the boat took off for the bay she watched the remaining rocks crash along the coastline. Had she been in danger from the landslide or saved by it? Ahmed was in the boat behind and she refused to look at it, fiddling with her blankets and murmuring, '*Merci, merci bien. Vouz m'excuse. Merci.*'

They reached the beach within minutes. A small crowd of

holiday makers craned their necks to watch: parents holding children, children holding beach balls. Daisy waded weakly through the shallow waves and obediently waited on the sand for instructions. She saw Ahmed jump from the boat ahead of his rescuers. She gave a nervous, exhausted wave, but he did not join her. When he reached the shore he suddenly took off, sprinting away from the astonished officials, across the beach and up to the cliff path. The men gestured to Daisy and one went off in uncertain pursuit. Then Daisy was taken to an ambulance waiting in the car park. There were two crew members and the woman said she would give Daisy a quick check over. They both had a kind of swagger and were quite good-looking, maybe because their uniforms were a bit more flattering than those in England. And they were slim, like in a film. Which, come to think of it, Daisy's life was beginning to resemble: a cliff disaster, a psycho who had saved her life and everyone in nice costumes. Daisy really hoped she didn't have any internal bleeding or missing limbs she hadn't noticed, because so long as she didn't, this was going to be quite a story to tell at school. And what would Toby think? Then she passed out.

Ten

Jenny had planned her sunbathing regime meticulously. Ten minutes of facial exposure (factor 30), an hour for the rest (factor 12) increasing by fifteen minutes a day. Two days off for sightseeing and shopping. That way she could be sure of a golden, lasting glow, without ageing effects.

A side effect of one heart attack, one near-death experience, fleeing guests and a working relationship with Provence's emergency services, was that her sunbathing timetable was in ruins. She had sat in the glare of the midday sun on several occasions and was as patchily red and white as a Spanish eighteen to thirty holiday maker.

She glanced at the fierce light through the shutters. Maybe it was all for the best; the temperature outside would have defeated the most fastidious monitoring of her complexion. She looked at Daisy's feathery cheeks as she slept. There was something to be said for being plump, although Daisy could afford to drop a bit of weight. Convalescence wouldn't do her any harm. Jenny envied Daisy's ability to sleep her way out of trouble. You could do that when you were young and not responsible for running households.

Jenny had rung Daisy's mother and reassured her that there was no harm done and they may as well stick to their plans. She had weighed up whether it was easier to have Daisy's mother here, but had decided it only meant more work, and anyway Jenny was enjoying her role as Mother Courage. It made her feel calm and strong and centred. Of course, if Daisy had really wanted her mother Jenny would have driven to the airport and collected her and made up the extra bed and so on, but Daisy had only said, 'Not if it is too much trouble.' Jenny hoped Daisy wasn't just being polite. Not that there was anything wrong in just being polite, so long as you weren't building up negative feelings inside.

Jenny stroked Daisy's forehead fondly. She felt she should continue to sit by her bed in case she was needed, and because it put her at the heart of her household. She would have liked to have been able to read a magazine, but it would make her seem less vital if Richard looked in – you didn't see nurses reading *Allure*. She did some ankle rotations and pelvic-floor exercises instead.

There was a faint knock on the door. Jenny assumed a sorrowful smile as Richard stepped in, holding a mug of tea.

'Thought you might like this,' he said, handing it to her. After nearly ten years of marriage he didn't know she only drank lemon or herbal tea. She sighed and put it on the bedside table.

'Thank you, darling,' she whispered.

'How is she?' asked Richard, peering respectfully at Daisy's slumbering form.

'I think she is fine, so long as I am here. What's happening out there? Is Syrie looking after you?'

She tried to suppress the note of triumph in her question.

'She's putting some clothes in the machine. She asked if we needed anything doing. I found some of Emily's pants. Shall I take anything from our room?'

'Oh, don't worry, I'll do it later.'

'Don't wear yourself out,' said Richard, squeezing her shoulder.

It felt like her collar bone was being broken, but never mind. He did not have Ahmed's artistry. Where was he? Where? That was the other reason Jenny could not leave Daisy's side: Jessica Arnout had mentioned that the police would need to question Daisy about Ahmed. He was in trouble, but Jenny could not find out why without arousing suspicion. She knew he had been with Daisy. Of course he had; Jenny had asked him to follow her on her walk. Thank God she had, what with a murderer being on the loose. When Daisy was recovered and there was a big enough audience of family and friends, Jenny would reveal her role in saving Daisy. But why had Ahmed run away? What was he afraid of?

'Have you spoken to Jessica? Is she coming round?' she asked Richard fretfully.

'No, she hasn't been in touch,' said Richard. 'Do you want me to get hold of her?'

'Well, yes. I thought I'd asked you. Perhaps you've been too busy,' said Jenny tightly.

'I'll try her mobile. You drink your tea.'

Jenny inhaled and exhaled, blocking off one nostril at a time. One had to impose internal calm on the external world. She was suddenly aware of Daisy's open-eyed interest.

'Hello, love, how are you feeling?'

Daisy yawned without putting her hand over her mouth.

'Fine. Where is everyone?'

The resilience of the young. They drained energy from their elders. Daisy shuffled her legs, so that one plump pink thigh pushed its way out of the duvet.

'Gosh, I must have slept for ever. What's happening? How's Dad?'

'He should be out of hospital tomorrow. We weren't sure who needed more looking after,' said Jenny, drawing implicit attention to the pastoral nature of her holiday.

'I hope we haven't been too much trouble,' said Daisy humbly. 'Maybe if Mum came out . . .'

'I bet you can't wait to get home,' said Jenny. 'Syrie has been on the internet looking for flights. Now, why don't you have a relaxing bath? I've popped some smellies by the basin and a nice big towel. Then you can come and have something to eat.'

'I'd prefer to jump in the pool,' said Daisy, 'if that's OK.'

'Why don't you have a relaxing bath first and a swim afterwards?' Jenny frowned. 'I always shower before using the pool, it's more hygienic.'

'OK,' said Daisy in a small voice.

'I'll leave you to it then,' said Jenny. She gave Daisy a finger wave and tiptoed from the room.

As she walked past the phone it suddenly rang, sounding like a fire alarm.

'Jesus!' cursed Jenny and then said a more dove-like 'Hi' into the receiver. Surely this must be Jessica, letting her know that her playmate Ahmed was OK and available for shoulder massages and painting instruction. Jenny felt hopeful tears rising. The holiday had become so melodramatic that her simple needs – a pale gold suntan and a man who admired her, seemed trivial. But she was trivial! There she had said it! Holidays were supposed to be trivial. But there was some fault line here. The emotional springs were spewing out lava instead of mineral water. If only she could rewind to that first evening. Gin and tonics, voices in the night air, nobody conked out, sweet Toby and her guardian gardener Ahmed. Perfect.

'So how is he?' she asked dreamily. 'Why did he run away like that?'

'What? How did you know it was me? Is that you, Jenny?

You sound so young. I thought it must be Daisy, but of course it can't be. Derek ... we ... didn't mean to run away. It was just that we'd promised ourselves a quiet break together this year and, looking back on it, we should never have accepted an invitation to holiday with other couples. But look, I am phoning to see if Daisy is OK. What a frightening experience for her. I don't quite understand how Ahmed fitted into it all? And is Daisy injured? It's a miracle if she is unhurt.'

Jenny looked at a large fly, which was using her hand gripping the receiver as a staging post to get on the wall. Was there anything more disappointing than the wrong person at the end of the phone? And with so many boring questions when Jenny wanted some answers. But Jenny's social sense was her guiding morality. One had to play nicely.

'Amanda! Fancy hearing from you. I thought you had given up on us. It's been awful. Awful for Daisy, but I've been sitting with her most of the time and I'm glad to say she is getting her strength back. A few bruises, but nothing worse. Amazingly.'

'Thank heavens for that,' said Amanda. 'I don't suppose she's well enough to speak to me yet?'

'Almost,' said Jenny lightly. 'But not quite yet. She's still depending on her nurse, who is yours truly for the moment. Oh, and you asked about Ahmed. It is very simple. He saved her life. Daisy would have been buried under rocks – entombed in fact, if it hadn't been for Ahmed.'

'Good Lord,' said Amanda. 'What a terrible image. But why did he run away afterwards?'

'Because he's shy,' said Jenny firmly. 'And now, if you'll excuse me, I had better get back to my patient.'

It was only after she had replaced the receiver on, frankly, an impertinent deserter, that she wondered how Amanda had known? Who among the guests here had she spoken to? Jenny fervently hoped that Syrie had not been snitching on the negative aspects of the holiday. After all Jenny had done for her and her Viagra victim.

Frankly, Jenny felt like climbing under a duvet herself. She'd need another holiday to recover from this one. She felt jittery and out of sorts. Where was sweet Ahmed? She strode out through the kitchen to the pool, like a ward sister taking a register.

Toby and Syrie were chatting and watching Emily dive for coins. Toby had his arms behind his head, while Syrie was kicking out her legs in front of her. Jenny was a reader of body language, indeed she had several books on the subject. Good heavens, they find each other attractive, she thought. As if she did not have enough to worry about.

'How's Daisy?' asked Toby.

'She's having a nice relaxing bath and then she'll be out,' said Jenny. 'You two look as if you're having a nice natter.'

'Toby has promised to take me parasailing,' said Syrie. Her oval face was animated, her eyes as bright as spotlights. She kicked away her novel. Flirtation was evidently marvellous for the spirits.

'Ooh, best leave that to the young,' said Jenny. 'Should we be thinking of supper?'

'You're always thinking of meals,' said Toby. He turned to Syrie. 'She keeps menus everywhere. She's like an online shopping service.'

'Well, somebody has to,' said Jenny, hurt. Toby had never used her as a butt of his jokes before. Relationships were so Darwinian. In order to bond, someone else had to be derided or excluded.

'Throw me some more money,' cried Emily.

Richard padded out, his shirt hanging over his shorts, his face mottled with heat or stress.

'I got through to Jessica,' he said.

'You're making too many phone calls,' said Jenny absent-mindedly. 'Is she coming over?'

'She suggested you drive over to her house.'

'Drive over to her? But I have so much to do here, and I don't know how to get to her house.'

'You can see it from here, it's not far,' said Richard. 'She said she was tied up.'

'Tied up?'

'Well, busy. She said she was busy.'

Emily surfaced from the pool.

'Throw some more coins, Dad. For my bank.'

'Everyone wants me for my money,' said Richard glumly. 'Here you go.'

Daisy came out, in a bikini with a T-shirt on top. She looked rested, plumped up like a cushion. Jenny feared that her own face was becoming gaunt. She had deep lines between her nose and mouth, just as Olivia Newton John did. Unless Olivia had been fixed. She had been thinking about a bit of repair work herself.

'You look so much better,' she said to Daisy. How the young bounced back. It was only the petty grind of decades that wore a face out.

'Hi, Tobes,' said Daisy shyly.

Toby got up and hugged her, his dark hair mingling with her mousy damp curls. Jenny looked slyly at Syrie.

'I'll come with you next time,' said Toby releasing himself from Daisy's puppyish hold.

Emily surveyed Daisy respectfully, her chin digging into her folded arms on the edge of the pool.

'How big was your dive?' she asked. 'Was it from the sky?'

'It felt like it,' said Daisy. 'Though Ahmed jumped from higher up. I'm amazed he survived.'

'Let's hope he did,' said Jenny harshly. She felt all eyes on her.

'We don't know where he is.'

'He was here,' said Emily.

'What? Where? When did you see him?' said Jenny.

'While you were inside with Daisy. He called to me from the fence. But he couldn't play with me today, he had to go.'

'Did he want to speak to me?' said Jenny.

'No, just me.'

'Did he ask where I was?'

'Yes, I said you were inside with Daisy. And he asked if Daisy was better and I said she had fallen off a cliff and that it was a serious matter, but she wasn't dead or you would be crying.'

'Why didn't you come to tell me?' said Jenny.

'Cos Dad said you weren't to be disturbed. And Ahmed said not to tell anyone I had seen him. I can keep secrets. But you looked so sad, Mummy, that I decided to tell you.'

'What was Ahmed doing by the cliff?' asked Toby.

Daisy looked at Jenny.

'That is what totally freaked me. He was hiding. He was following me.'

'I asked him to keep an eye on you,' said Jenny. She added dramatically and untruthfully, 'I had a premonition.'

'What's that?' asked Emily.

'It's when you guess that something is going to happen,' said Jenny.

'That's a prediction, a premonition is like a dream, the sort of things fortune tellers have,' said Syrie.

204

Christ, thought Jenny, I'd hoped the dictionary had gone with Amanda. Talk of fortune tellers made her seem common.

'Like Joan of Arc,' she said, fumbling for nibbles in a sweaty-looking bowl that had been left on the table since the night before.

'I was afraid of Ahmed,' said Daisy quietly.

'How can you be afraid of Ahmed?' said Emily indignantly. 'He's our friend.'

'There was all that shit in the newspapers about tourists being preyed on. And I thought, for a moment . . . that's why I went down the cliff path. To get away from him.'

Jenny felt her saliva turn sour. It was like the pool games she played with Emily, pretending to throw her in so she could rescue her. Got you, got you. So you were both threat and saviour. She looked round nervously. Damn, Richard was there.

'So, my interfering little wife was behind the mishap,' said Richard, banteringly. 'Never one to leave well alone.'

Jenny laughed, through tears.

'I can see when I'm not wanted. I'll go over to Jessica's. Do you have the car keys, darling?'

'Course you're wanted,' said Richard, extending a large damp arm towards her, like a whale fin.

Jenny felt her insides closing and knotting. She brushed past him, swept the keys up from the kitchen sideboard and trotted out of the house. She would have sobbed if she had not been concerned about her mascara. Her nose was dribbling as she altered the seat and the mirror and jerked the car forward in a haze of exhaust fumes.

Jessica's house was easy to find. It was a smaller version of the villa, slightly prettier and far easier to manage. The sort of house one might choose for a holiday if you wanted an intimate family gathering rather than running a major A and E department.

'Pull yourself together, Jenny,' she said fiercely to her reflection in the wing mirror. 'Half full rather than half empty, remember. Breathe.' Her large, sad, blue eyes looked back at her and her mouth moved into a welcoming smile.

'Sorry, sorry,' she said before Jessica had opened the door. 'I should have brought flowers.'

Jessica was smiling through a garland of smoke.

'My dear,' she said. She was wearing a lilac and gold kaftan, her hair swept up behind her. She looked like Virginia, if Virgina had run off with Serge Gainsbourg.

Everything smelt of her – her clothes, her house – of flowers, nutmeg and smoke, an enticing mix. Jenny offered her cheek for her three sharp kisses but, instead, Jessica kissed her on her lips.

'It is my custom,' she said with a shrug.

Jenny thought, How sophisticated, and wondered if it should become her custom too. That would wipe the cat's smile from Syrie's face.

'Ooh, what pretty chair covers,' she said, peeping into the small sitting room, which was full of wood and lace. On the table was a jug of iced water and some fruit tart. The jug and plates were of a striking design, a blue background decorated with red-brown figs. In the corner, was Ahmed.

'Oh, it's you,' she breathed.

Ahmed got up and limped towards her. Jenny held out her hand to him and he took it, pressing her fingers as she spoke.

'Why did you run away?'

Ahmed glanced at Jessica Arnout and then back to Jenny. His thin, handsome face fell.

'Because I have no papers, and I don't want to go back to Algeria.'

'But you are not doing anyone any harm! Why shoudn't you stay here?' said Jenny, enjoying the sound of her human rights indignation. Let's see what Syrie made of her championing of the dispossessed. She wouldn't patronize her now. But it wasn't only a pleasing self-righteousness that made Jenny cry out. There was also the rough sensation of Ahmed's hand, like a cat's tongue, on hers, sending signals along the telephone wires of her arm, stomach and pelvis. 'I was worried about you,' she said.

She felt flushed and crackling. She had not expected romance here. When she had brushed the back of her hand against Ahmed's groin during a painting session it had been a gesture of anxious lust rather than romance. She had felt lonely and

207

ignored. There were always other reasons for sex. She wondered what sort of relationship would follow sex with Ahmed.

What was a relationship anyway? Talking only mattered to those who were conversationally inclined. She and Richard traded information rather than ideas or feelings, but then so did most people. No, it wasn't so much sex and then the rest. It was how to eke out the quality of sex once sex had lost its quality. When Jenny started her affair with Richard she felt she had been given a code to him. Physical intimacy had bestowed sympathy and understanding, but there had been no progression beyond sex. The longer Jenny had known Richard the more stranded their marriage seemed. There was a form to it, but no engine.

With Ahmed there was no barrier of shared language and trapped togetherness. Patently he respected and desired Jenny and a flattering self-image is the most powerful aphrodisiac. He was her spiritual renewal, her holiday.

'Shall we take a walk?' said Jenny.

Ahmed shoved his hands into his back pockets and followed her to the door. Then he hung back.

'I stay here, inside. For me, it is better,' he said, looking down at Jenny's feet.

Jenny, in turn, peered at his open shirt. What she wanted was an hour of light, flirtatious sex. She wanted to be kissed and fondled, but definitely not made pregnant.

'I want the starter but not the main course or the pudding,' she said.

'Pardon?'

Ha, ha, ha, she thought. I am mistress in my own language. What was the inscription in that political biography Amanda had left for Syrie? Power without responsibility. Surprisingly good advice from an accountant. Why hadn't Syrie looked more chuffed? The last time Jenny had had an affair she had been powerless. It had taken a baby to smash the family unit. This time it was different. She *was* the family unit, she was a woman of substance. Why not enjoy it? She was better than Olivia Newton John. She was Anna bloody Karenina.

'You are hungry?' asked Ahmed, his shoulders hunched.

'For you,' murmured Jenny, plucking at his lips, which felt dry and strange. His breath smelt of aniseed. As they embraced she arched and tipped her head backwards. It was very pleasurable to be touched by unfamiliar hands, and the feeling was heightened when watched by eyes hidden behind a cloud of smoke. She remembered that illicit sex was sudden and furtive. Language was a further obstacle to prolonged court-ship. He unfastened his belt and was upon her.

Jenny left the house with a promise to return the following day.

Arriving back at the villa she found everyone in the same position, unchanged, while she, Narnia like, had been hiding in the wardrobe.

'Hi, darling,' said Richard, opening one eye as he lay on his back by the pool, his stomach mountainously rising and falling.

Jenny lit one of Toby's cigarettes. She blew the smoke vertically out of her mouth from the launch pad of her lower lip. It was a post-coital gesture. There were about a hundred signs that people had had sex. It might as well be written on her forehead, she thought, as she turned her collar outwards and smoothed her hair. Was Richard blind? Ah, no more than any of us. What is trust except turning your back on the hundred signs?

'So what are you all hanging around for?' she asked. (There were also the personality altering effects of sex. I'm not Olivia Newton John or Anna Karenina, thought Jenny. I am Katie Hepburn!)

'We're going to fetch Dad,' Daisy said tentatively. 'We were just waiting for you to tell you where we'd gone.'

Jenny blinked rapidly.

'Yes, of course, sorry, I got held up.'

'That's OK.' Daisy shrugged. The pink of her shoulders was accentuated by the white line from her bra strap. 'It's not like he has a lot of appointments.'

Syrie gave a soft groan.

'Nothing more powerless than a sick man, right? All the staff and the diaries and the conference calls in the world can't help you.'

'That's only one side of him,' said Daisy, tracing a plump

finger along the wall. Jenny hated it when people got their hands needlessly dirty.

'Believe me, the office is his personality,' said Syrie. 'I don't know what to say to him: shall I say everybody has called, which will just make him jumpy; or nobody has called, which will make him paranoid?'

'Which is true?' asked Richard.

'Depends on the vibe,' said Syrie.

Richard looked at Daisy. 'What does that mean? I only speak English as a first language.' He chortled.

'Do you think we could go now?' asked Daisy anxiously.

Jenny stayed behind, completing small domestic tasks to pass the time: pushing her fist into cushions, refilling the ice box, emptying the wastepaper bins. She caught sight of her reflection in the mirror and widened her eyes conspiratorially. Outside, Toby was dragging garden furniture around, a handkerchief on his head and his surfer bathing trunks low on his tawny hips. Unimprovable, thought Jenny, fondly. The clock should stop here, before the erosion begins. She felt suddenly mournful about the vast gap between herself now and herself at Toby's age. There was so much to look back on. Toby was all potential and she was all past. Growing old meant giving up your role as centre of your universe for a cameo part. Just one last time! thought Jenny. One last chance to feel vivid. There was something marvellously redemptive about an affair.

'It's just a tonic,' she said to her reflection. 'It'll put a bit of zip back into my marriage. Makes me feel appreciated.' She smiled and immediately winced at the web of lines around her eyes and mouth. She brought her hands together in front of her face.

'Just for now, and then I'll be good,' she whispered. 'Dear God, let nobody find out and my marriage last. I just need a week or so. I'll work it off. I'll make it up. Thank you, God. For you are the one true God and I am but a miserable sinner.'

'Talking to yourself?' Toby poked his head around the door.

That was the thing with the young, they moved so fast, like panthers.

'I was just calling Emily. Have you seen her?'

'Er, yeah. She went looking for you when you hadn't come back from Jessica's. You must have missed each other. She's probably there by now. You want to ring?'

'Um, why don't you? The number is on the table.'

'Oh. OK. I can speak in English, right?'

'Yes, of course.'

'And if Em is there, you want to speak to her?'

'Oh, I'm sure she would rather speak to you.'

'Um. And then should I fetch her?'

'Oh, would you?'

Toby pulled a T-shirt over his head and went to make the phone call. A few minutes later he left the house whistling. Jenny breathed out. The thing is, she thought, I love Emily so much. But I can't take her chatter just now, I need some privacy. A temporary seclusion zone.

It was also a matter of good taste. Only a very slutty sort of woman could embrace her children and her lover. One had to choose. One could not satisfy both. However, the choice was not either/or but now and later. There was an urgency to sexual love, but maternal love was infinite and therefore probably OK to put on hold. When thoughts began to crowd in on Jenny like this she knew how to respond. She pulled out her lavender sweat pants and tight cropped T-shirt, tied the laces on her Air Max trainers and started bouncing on the spot with little hisses of exhaled breath. Then she ran and she ran and she ran.

As Jenny returned up the drive, her limbs trembling with heat and exhaustion, her head drooping rather than nodding in the Paula Radcliff fashion to which she imaginatively aspired, she saw the car was back, and the front door open. Inside would be the cast list of her life and she would have to assume her role as solicitous friend to Gerry and hostess and mother. The solid claims of this community made her gasp. She bent double to relieve the nausea, her hands swinging in the dust. She wiped her mouth and felt dry grit on her gums. Very well, back to your fat but faithful husband, your ravenous daughter, those self-righteous teenagers, the sick man and his floozy. Back you go, Jenny.

She paced round the side of the house and surveyed the group, hands on hips, pools of sweat round her midriff.

'Mummy,' said Emily running up and taking her hand. 'Isn't it good that Gerry is back? But we have to be quiet and look after him very well.'

'Yes, isn't it? And thank you for coming to look for me. Did Jessica tell you I had already left?' asked Jenny, cat's cradling Emily's fingers between her own.

'Ahmed did. He's staying there you know. He said I should come back there tomorrow with you and we can make pottery animals. For my friends. Jessica said she would help me, because Ahmed was working on something special with you. What are you doing, Mummy? I prefer Ahmed, because Jessica smells of old smoke and I don't think she can even paint. Couldn't you work on your special thing with her, so I could do animals with Ahmed?'

'Can you girls stop your chattering for a minute?' called Richard. 'Come over here so we can have a toast to Gerry. Fewer birds, more birdies is my advice!'

'Less birds,' said Jenny firmly. 'Once a PA, always a PA. I'm still having to correct his grammar!'

Gerry, who looked dreadful, his skin folding around his face and his neck like an old turkey's, raised his glass.

'Fewer, less. What the hell.'

'Fewer!' said Syrie, who had changed into a floaty pink evening dress and applied some pearly lipstick.

'Less,' said Jenny, grabbing a glass of champagne and waving it at Toby.

'To life! Thank God,' he responded, handing a glass to Daisy.

What an extremely grown-up toast thought Jenny. One spends so long indulging children by treating them as adults – Would you like a glass of wine? What do *you* think of whatever thing they can only barely understand – and then, Christ, they really are adult.

'So, Jenny have you been looking after everyone while I've been away?' said Gerry, in a manner that would have been suave if his skin did not hang like washing over his frame. How could weight loss change a character so? Jenny gave silent thanks to God that she had avoided crash diets, even before a holiday.

What Gerry meant of course was had Jenny been looking after Syrie and Daisy who he called, inaccurately in the plural, his girls. He looked from one to the other with pathetic devotion. Not so sure of their love any more, not so sure he was lovable. Jenny felt post-coitally athletic and commanding. It was shocking how power could change hands. Now she could condescend to Gerry because he was enfeebled and probably impotent. She felt sexier than Syrie, wiser than Daisy, more pivotal than Richard. She had forgotten how confidence-boosting an affair was. It was like assuming the gladiator position in yoga, except it lasted longer and obviously you were on your back and mobile rather than upright and still.

She picked up a bowl of crisps from the table and offered them round. 'Yes, of course I've been looking after everyone, Gerry,' she said, enjoying the sound of her own voice, the swish of her dress against her legs. She was better than Olivia Newton John. She was Marilyn Monroe.

The next day Jenny went to seek Jessica's advice about local crafts, the day after that she drove over to report a grey tinge to the swimming pool ('Maybe it's just that the weather is cloudy,' suggested Toby gently). The following afternoon she nipped off to check the weather reports and also to see whether the region's killer had struck again after Gerry idly mentioned it over lunch.

'Jenny, sit down,' said Gerry, waving weakly across the table. He had not lost the sunless quality to his skin – it was the colour of the earth beneath a lifted log – but his eyes no longer looked fearful. Jenny noticed, to her surprise, that his other hand was clasped in Syrie's under the table. Somehow furtive affection was more shocking than sex. Jenny's main thought these days was how to make her escape from them all. But she had sensed a developing quietness and calmness among all of them as they became, well, more considerate.

Syrie did not jangle in the same way, Richard was solid rather than boorish, Toby and Daisy were more open, Emily less demanding. If Jenny had not been having an affair, she would have really started to enjoy the company. But instead, she was thin, nervy and excitable. There would be time enough for the placid kindness of friends and family. She just wanted a few more days of sweating and shuddering her way into a renewal. Just for now, while God's back was turned.

'I won't be long. I have to find out, don't you think? The killer might be outside the gates waiting to strike!'

'Did you say killer, Mummy?' asked Emily who was drawing on Daisy's sketchpad. 'I'm scared, if a killer is coming.'

'She was joking, Ems,' said Daisy leaning sideways. She was putting on weight, Jenny thought, before she could stop herself.

'Of course I was, darling. I won't be long.'

'You always say that, but then you are,' said Richard as a matter of fact rather than as a reproach.

'What's Jessica got that we haven't?' asked Gerry cheerfully.

Jenny laughed again and rose.

'Emily is making you a card,' said Daisy. 'You look as if you are wearing an evening dress in the picture. Why is your mummy in an evening dress, Em?'

'Because she looks pretty and she is going to meet someone,' said Emily, chewing at her pencil.

'I must go, darling. Show me when I get back.' Jenny waved.

'Who is Mummy going to meet?' asked Daisy.

'The killer,' said Emily, frowning.

Jessica and Ahmed were examining a broken vine at the side of the house when Jenny arrived. They spoke in a guttural French that was hard for Jenny to translate. It was not just the accent, it was the speed and fluency of the language. Jenny did not see how she would ever understand unless the French spoke more slowly, using a narrow vocabulary and leaving a space in which to reply. Funny how the barely educated Ahmed could master French so easily and was now passable at English. A talent for languages must be God's gift to the third-world nations, thought Jenny. She approached the couple shyly. She had not hidden her relationship with Ahmed – it was hard to explain away an hour with a man in the spare room – but neither had she explicitly discussed it with Jessica. She did not know how to explain either in French or English. She rather relied on Jessica's worldliness.

But this particular afternoon was different. When Jessica and Ahmed caught sight of Jenny standing back, scratching her arms, they exchanged glances and broke off their conversation.

'She arrives.' Jessica smiled. Ahmed lifted his arms slowly and strangely as if to Allah.

'Here, have some cold water,' said Jessica, pouring from the jug. Jenny took it eagerly, grateful for distracting props. Jessica was good to her, but intimidating.

'It tastes minty,' said Jenny, smiling.

Jessica nodded sagely. 'It is fresh, like you.'

'I thought I would just pop in,' said Jenny, taking a step forward. Ahmed walked towards her and locked his arms round her. She felt his aniseed breath on her neck and his unfashionably long hair tickling her shoulder. There was a lightness to him that still surprised her. If she had to describe Ahmed, she would have said honestly that he was unlike Richard.

'Ahmed has something to say to you, Jenny,' prompted Jessica turning to attend to her vine.

Ahmed gulped and took Jenny's face in his cupped hands, catching and pulling strands of her hair so that she thrust her head forward like a pony.

'Jenny, I want to tell you about our life together,' he said sadly. His pupils were as deep and dark as mines and, at such close range, the whites of his eyes were tinted with sulphur yellow.

'What are you talking about?' Jenny giggled. 'I don't think this is quite the time or the place . . .'

'When is the right time? Where is the right place to speak of love?' murmured Jessica straightening the stem of the vine which flopped brokenly to the ground when her hand moved. She sighed and held it erect on her arm. 'Continue, Ahmed.'

Ahmed gave her a quizzical glance, and then gripped Jenny more securely. 'I will stay where you are and you will go where I go,' he said.

Jenny wriggled away from him.

'Hang on, hang on,' she said. Go where? she thought, To Algeria? With no money? Her mind felt strange and spongy. It was hard to concentrate, to think or plan clearly. What does it matter? she asked herself. Another voice in her head replied, Because you only get one shot at this, Jenny. It is a lifetime of regret either way.

Wasn't permanent adventure a kind of torment? The point about holidays was that they were artificial adventures – you travelled thousands of miles but avoided discomfort or unpredictability and, above all, local populations. What Ahmed wanted was the opposite, the reality of foreignness which, on the whole, was about poverty.

'How could we live?' she asked, her hands fluttering away from his.

'We have a journey, like this,' he said, catching her hand and holding it to his chest. 'Inside here.'

'But I will become ugly and old,' she whimpered.

Ahmed jerked his head at Jessica. She spoke to him in French.

'You are beautiful,' he said to Jenny. 'Because I love you.'

Jenny wondered if this could be true. After the first rush of sex with Richard she had tended to make her own assessments of her attractiveness, depending on how much money and time she had spent on herself and whether she had slept well. That was the prosaic truth. Beauty was not in the eye of the beholder it was in the reflection of the mirror.

She sighed.

'I have my family,' she said.

Ahmed winked at her.

'I give you many babies,' he said.

Oh Lord, one was trouble enough. Turn back, Jenny. Go home.

Jessica gave a throaty chuckle.

'Freedom or the family,' she said. 'It is the big choice: love or duty.'

'You can have both,' said Jenny peevishly.

'Here, you are yourself,' said Jessica dramatically. 'You are born, you die. Alone. The family, it is – an illusion. It is not permanent. It survives without you, you survive without it.'

If there was a weakness in Jenny's nature, it was a desire to please. She wanted Jessica's good opinion. She wanted Ahmed to think her brave and free. Her head swam. What did it matter either way? She would make someone cross whatever she did.

'I will come with you.' She began to sob, spilling back into Ahmed's arms.

'Good,' said Jessica, lighting a cigarette. 'Have something to drink and then we will go to retrieve your clothes from the villa.'

Jenny felt as if the decision had been taken away from her and also the responsibility. She held her tumbler of lemon juice like a child, and gazed at Ahmed over the brim. Conversation with him amounted to less than the liquid language of his dark eyes. She felt singled out, hypnotized by this couple. She was cared for rather than caring. The trouble with her own family was that she did not truly believe they wanted her. Nobody had actively chosen her. Ahmed's eyes and his prick were calling her, renewing her. Jessica was the siren who had brought her here.

'Are you ready?' asked Jessica, tapping her bare foot. 'We will go.'

They drove in silence over the bumpy track. Jenny did not want to risk forfeiting this woman's approval with supplementary questions. Instead, she politely looked out of the window at the drooping sunflowers and broken-down fences and a circle of stones strewn with ashes. Summer tired so quickly, there was no freshness left, everything, everyone had been out in the sun too long.

Jenny felt as if she had a rodent in her stomach. She exhaled behind a cupped hand. Jessica, looking straight ahead, reached across and took Jenny's hand in her sun-lined, nicotine-stained but still soft fingers. Jenny held on tight as they approached the villa. Jessica must act as a barrister for her. Richard could be frightening if he were displeased. Still, it was his fault for not loving her enough.

'Is my little wife interfering again?' She remembered his words like a fresh slap. She was not a bolter; she was a woman with a grievance. It was not her fault. It was not her fault.

'It is not your fault,' said Jessica as she pulled on the steering wheel.

'But I have been unfaithful,' gasped Jenny.

'And Richard hasn't?' Jessica smirked. 'Open your eyes.'

Jenny felt momentarily dazed. She had imagined herself in the role of romantic heroine turning her back on her unappreciative but steadfast husband. It was not a new life she was choosing so much as a grand scene. If Richard showed enough anguish and remorse then she was prepared to reconsider. But what if her marriage were simply worn out so the only stimulation lay outside it? The thought struck her like a brick. Richard was as disappointed with her as she was with him. It was not work or money that made him irritable. It was her.

'What do you mean? Who has Richard been unfaithful

with?' She straightened her back and repeated with elaborate dignity. 'I mean, with whom has he had an affair? Syrie?'

Jessica narrowed her eyes and yanked the gear stick as she juddered along the drive towards the villa.

'Amanda, sure, he has had an affair with her. I don't know yet of Syrie. I don't think so. Maybe later.'

Jenny screwed up her face in misery.

'Amanda's my friend,' she said quivering.

'Always that is true, no?' said Jessica. 'People make love with husbands of friends. Love happens among people as also betrayal and murder. Why would you want to have the affair or to kill someone you do not know? It is not sensible, is it?'

'Amanda,' said Jenny. 'Trying to make everyone sorry for her. She abused our sympathy, that's what she did. I thought, poor Amanda with her crippled husband, and meanwhile she was getting her claws into my husband.'

'Her claws? Like the bird? Yes, I see. Well, what can one say? Perhaps Amanda did not want you to feel sorry for her. Maybe she thought she would rather make you jealous. But you know, I guess it was not about you. Neither Amanda nor Richard were thinking about you.'

'Couldn't even look me in the eye,' said Jenny pinching her lips. 'Just took my hospitality and destroyed my marriage. Because she was unhappy.'

'Yes,' said Jessica impatiently. 'Nobody knows about ownership any more. They want what isn't theirs. They want to rent. Husbands, villas, you know.'

'Having an affair is hardly the same as renting a villa,' snorted Jenny. 'Look at me, I am shaking. I cannot believe this has happened.'

'*Alors*,' said Jessica, throwing back her head. 'It is true, your husband, your friend, they have done something monstrous.That is why you must leave. You must leave in order to be safe. Your husband is a danger to you now, no? I can give you . . . a refuge from your terrible life.'

'I have to go. There's no question. After what Richard and she have done to me. Help me, Jessica. Help me do what is right. God give me strength . . .'

'Richard! Richard!' she called.

The house was empty. She would have to pack her case and leave a note. Relieved and disappointed, she went to her bedroom and began pulling dresses from their hangers. She loved packing, now more than ever.

As she lined her case with tissue she heard voices outside. She hesitated and then, heart jangling, walked to the terrace. Toby and Jessica were standing opposite each other, both with their arms folded.

'What's going on?' asked Toby.

'Ask your mother-in-law,' said Jessica, blowing a smoke ring.

'Step-mother,' said Jenny brightly. 'Where is everyone?'

'They've taken Gerry to get some sea air,' said Toby. 'Emily went too so she could add some dolphins and whales to her card. Oh, and mermaids.'

Thank God, thought Jenny. She could not quite square Emily . . .

'Toby, I am going away for a while,' said Jenny fastening her eyes on a small white cloud in the shape of a yacht.

He moved into view, standing in front of her like a lifeguard.

'Jessica said.'

'*Alors*, enough explanation,' said Jessica gaily. 'Some things, from the heart, cannot be explained. Better go.'

She took Jenny's arm and propelled her back to the house. But Toby moved again, to block the way.

'Could I have a word with you alone?' he said.

Jessica shrugged. 'I will complete the packing,' she whispered to Jenny.

Jenny frowned. She did not want her belongings packed any old how. And she did not want to be alone with Toby. She was frightened by his aggressive behaviour. He was always so graceful and relaxed. He did not make scenes. Jenny thought somehow that he would wave her off as lightly as he had accepted her. They would still see each other. Chill Toby, she said to herself. Let's all just chill.

She sat down sulkily on a chair.

'What is it you wanted to say?'

He waited until Jessica had gone, then pulled a chair in front of her, turning it round so he leaned over the high wooden slats. His upper arms formed hillocks even when folded and flattened across the top of the chair. Jenny blinked and saw him perched in a large chair, wearing his school uniform. She blinked again as the dark eyes and spider lashes stared back at her in a different face, rougher, thinner and stubble-chinned.

'Toby? This isn't the time. What is it?'

'Only this: don't go.'

'But why? You don't need me here.'

He did not answer this question.

'Sometimes you have to stay,' he said. 'You can't keep messing everyone up.'

Jenny felt hot and tearful.

'Oh, I know you blame me, everyone blames me. That's why it is better that I go.'

'I wasn't thinking about you. I was thinking about Emily. What's left of this family. What is it with your generation that you can't make a commitment?'

Jenny flinched.

'I don't know what you are talking about. You're too young to judge these things Toby, you don't understand about adult emotions. It is not as simple as you think. Richard . . .'

'I understand that you all fuck up all the time,' he said, taking one of Jessica's cigarettes and a lighter from the table.

'Don't smoke, Toby. You musn't start smoking. It's very bad for you.'

'Like, you care? You're not even going to be here.'

'That's not the point. Trying to make me feel guilty won't help. You can't punish me by smoking a cigarette.'

'So what else can I do? And why doesn't it help to make you feel guilty? You should feel guilty. You should feel like shit.'

'You don't know. One day you might judge things differently,' she said.

'Yeah, one day. I'm talking about this day.'

'Be positive, Toby,' said Jenny uneasily. 'We all have to find ourselves. There is no point in me being here if I am not fulfilled. I need a husband who appreciates me. Richard – well, I don't have to say any more. I cannot be happy in the current situation.'

'Why not? Who gives a shit? Emily doesn't want you to be fulfilled; she just wants you to be her mum. You are so selfish, so selfish.'

'This isn't helpful,' said Jenny standing up. 'You must understand that I want to be free,'

'Free from what?' shouted Toby. 'Free for what? Since when is the chance of a shag the same thing as freedom? Your freedom is just a refusal to take responsibility. You are full of shit.'

'Stop that, stop that language,' said Jenny. 'You aren't my family. You belong to Richard and Virginia. Do you know what I think? I think Emily belongs to Richard and Virginia too. She never warmed to me. It was all a mistake. I had no right to have her, Richard made that clear. He never wanted her and he never wanted me.'

Toby was silent. Taut-faced, appalled, he stared past her. Jenny turned to see what apparition had transfixed him. Richard and Emily were standing behind her.

Eleven

A Year Later

The package slid onto the stone floor of Jenny's home. She put down her dustpan and brush and ran to take a look. Her rough brown hands fondled the polythene wrapper. It was addressed to Madam Arnout. Jessica's voice called irritably from the kitchen.

'Jennifer, why can't you finish the job before you look at the post? We have a busy day. The villa still has to be prepared, I need you to take these provisions down to stock the fridge. Is that the right verb, to stock?'

'I was expecting something, that's all,' said Jenny, wiping her hands on her cheap housecoat. She could feel her hip bones through the material. The coat hanger, Ahmed had sneered. No tits at all.

At least there had been civility in Richard's lovelessness. For someone who spoke English as a second language, Ahmed used some startlingly precise insults. But then Jenny embodied his disappointment.

Ahmed was confused and angry; he had shouted at Jenny that morning. Jessica had said to him that Jenny was a nice lady and would give him a passport and money. But now he felt used. Jenny wasn't a nice lady; she was a bit of a slut. And she had no heart; she did not mind being without her daughter. She was a bad mother. And she had no tits.

It had been fine at the start. Jenny had a pretty face and looked as if she was going to cry. That great oaf of a husband with his loud voice and pumpkin head – he had made Jenny sad. Ahmed could see that. She didn't feel beautiful, and a woman must be cherished. Unless she turned out to be a whore.

Why did Jenny want to leave her daughter? She was a good little girl; she had trusted him. She wasn't a racist buffoon like her father.

Ahmed had been happy when Emily had opened his shed door, as quiet as the breeze, and had sat herself down on the bench and begun moulding the clay with her small, sure fingers. She was a self-possessed little girl. If she were his daughter, he could not leave her. So he could not forgive Emily's mother for her desertion, even though he was the cause of it.

He was angry with these lustful old women and longed for a shy virgin he could confidently call his own. He was tired of Jessica's games. He thought he was supposed to be her lover. He had made everything good for her, but she was a little bit crazy. He thought she fancied Jenny for herself. She wanted him to procure women for her. Any tourist would do. That was not a way to live. It was not a way to die.

And now he was landed with Jenny, just when his mother had sent him a picture of the girl. He took it out and examined it. He screwed up his eyes. A sweet, honest girl, a modest girl. She would be a good mother. And she had big tits. Ahmed sighed with irritation and guilt. He didn't want to hurt Jenny. It was a bloody awful situation, and he had been tricked into it. To hell with the passport. He could make a living back home somehow, and be among decent people. His mother wanted him back. He didn't want his prick worn out by these bitches. His head felt compressed and overheated. He was going to raise his arm to one of them, unless they watched their step.

Looking back, Jenny realized there had only been one moment of absolute sympathy, call it love, between her and Ahmed. That was the moment she had submitted to his proposal by the vine in front of Jessica. The price she had paid for that fleeting sensation of sunshine and fluidity had been formidable: her child, her husband, her security, her beauty, her anxious pleasures in life, Ahmed's respect and gentleness. She regretted her decision immediately she had made it, perhaps before. Every day she regretted it more.

A decision was too strong a word. It had been more of an impulse buy. It had been such a terrifying whim, Jenny believed she must have been ill at the time. She had to plead some kind of mitigation if only to get her sentence reduced.

After a few weeks of living with Ahmed Jenny felt emotionally bored and then disgusted. She packed her bag and phoned home, but there was something wrong with the line and she could not get a connection. She phoned Richard at work but his secretary said, after drawing in her breath that Richard was in a meeting. Jenny then tried Amanda and got through.

'Jenny?' said Amanda, shocked.

'Yes, hey, surprise! Did you think I had disappeared off the face of the earth?' said Jenny, talking as fast as her heart was beating.

'No, I knew where you were.'

There was a pause. Jenny could hear the windows rattling behind her and felt foreboding in the wind and in the voice on the other end of the phone.

'I think I'll come home now,' Jenny said, wondering at the conviction in her voice. 'I've made a mistake.'

The back door slammed shut. She looked round and there was Ahmed, holding several stalks of sunflowers, his expression shifty and remorseful. Jenny shook with shock and conflict. Ahmed looked so young and sorry, like Toby, who when he was a small boy had ridden his bike over the new hall carpet (before she had wooden floors, of course, which changed everything). She had shouted at him and he had let the bike fall and run off, the spokes of the front wheel still turning in slow motion. Later, he had returned with some some scraggy, dog-shitty dandelions as a peace offering, bless him.

She should forgive Ahmed just as she had forgiven Toby. Ahmed depended on her, probably cared for her more than she gave him credit for. It was the situation that had made him lose his temper: not having their own place; not having any bloody money. Relationships can survive betrayal or indifference, but poverty is a challenge too far.

Home suddenly assumed a greater aura of unreality, and guilt. Jenny would be in the wrong for ever.

'Have you spoken to Richard?' asked Amanda, disapproval racing down the telephone wire.

'No, I'll leave that to you,' said Jenny.

'Sorry?'

Jenny held out her hand to Ahmed.

'You heard me. You want him, you have him.'

'Jenny, what is wrong with you? What on earth are you doing? Don't you know that Emily—'

'Don't. Don't. Don't. Don't. Don't. Leave me alone,' said Jenny.

'Jenny, you phoned me.'

'Yes, social call. Ha, ha. Must go. Look after them for me. Everyone benefits from this, everyone benefits. Much better to have me out of the way, eh?'

She carefully replaced the receiver on Amanda's babbling, hypocritical indignation. Her breathing became raucous and asthmatic. She grabbed Ahmed.

'There, there. Don't worry, little girl, I will look after you,' he said.

It was for the strong to protect the weak, thought Ahmed. He stroked Jenny's hair and shut his eyes. In his mind was the smiling, bashful girl in the photograph.

'We will make a clean start,' Ahmed said as he presented her with the flowers and some freshly painted breakfast bowls. But regret clung to their relationship like smog.

As if their mutual vocabulary were not strained enough, a whole range of subjects were out of bounds: home, family, the future. In the first few weeks they had talked about desire, but after that they usually talked about money. Richard used to be irritable about money, but that was from a position of having it – there had been a solid economic foundation. Jenny and Ahmed were like drowning swimmers.

The lifebelt to which they both clung was Jessica. She gave

them shelter and, humiliatingly, small change in return for work round the house. Jenny slid the money into the pocket of a grubby dress as if it were a strange kind of joke.

'Thank you for my dinner money,' she said, stretching her lips. 'Richard will sort this out with you.'

Jessica's laugh turned into a loose, phlegmy cough.

One evening Jenny opened the drawer next to the lopsided bed she shared with Ahmed and counted out the coins there. She needed some Tampax and did not have quite enough money herself. The small change which was once scattered round her home in Chiswick, behind sofa cushions, on mantelpieces, in coat pockets was now what she was living on. When Richard used to say they had no money, he had obviously not meant it in a literal sense. There had always been access to money. But Jenny's five euro were literally all she had, and it was not enough to buy Tampax. She sat on the bed, shoulders drooping and looked out of the window distractedly.

Could she use lavatory paper? She would have to get up several times during the night to check she was not leaking, but she didn't sleep well anyway.

Her thoughts moved like train tracks over her life here. She could not forget her visit to the bank in Marseille. She had worn a cocktail dress and had swept up her hair, assuming the brittle patience of a woman backed by a high-earning husband. She guessed she would have to explain, perhaps repeatedly, the slight complication of her situation: her own account, it was true, was overdrawn, but she had an arrangement with her husband to top it up. Funds would follow. Her bank was familiar with the idiosyncrasies of cash flow and would certainly sanction a temporary loan. A queue formed behind her with heavy sighs and gesticulation. Jenny tapped her fingers on the ledge to make clear that it was the obtuseness of the bank rather than any inadequacy of hers. Then she stopped because she realized she was moving her fingers as if across a computer keyboard. She shrugged at the man behind her in a what-can-you-do? sort of way, but he held up his newspaper in front of his face.

It turned out that it was not the language barrier nor provincial slow-wittedness that prevented the bank from cashing a cheque for her. It was a bar on her account. She had been cut adrift. She walked out of the bank smiling, her insides a mine shaft of terror. Jessica was standing on the other side of the street with her sunglasses on her head and her arms folded.

Jenny shut her eyes and gave a little shake of her head to clear the water in her ears that had been accumulating through the summer. When she opened her eyes she saw Ahmed looking at her through the window. The light was against him, so he pressed his face to the pane with a shielding hand.

'What you doing?' he mouthed.

Jenny looked around her. Ahmed's drawer was pulled wide open and her hand was suspended on the edge of it, digging for coins among the papers and letters, which may have been from his mother or indeed from his wife, for all Jenny cared.

Ahmed's face moved and she listened to his light steps along the side of the house. She waited listlessly. What was the point?

Ahmed's lightness had been the quality that had attracted her to him. It was the defining contrast with her husband. Ahmed's slim build and soft-footedness was like sunlight to Jenny, whereas Richard cast the shadow of an ancient oak. Yet she soon found there was something creepy about Ahmed's soundlessness. He approached her like a burglar, like a murderer. He slid through the door and held Jenny's wrist between his thumb and first finger. His grip was as tight as wire.

'What were you doing with my things, Jenny?' he said quietly. The use of her name, formerly a sign of intimacy was now used to imply coldness. 'Jenny' was not an endearment.

'I needed some money to buy some fucking Tampax,' she replied, yanking back her hand.

'Do not use that word. It is not feminine, not nice,' said Ahmed folding his arms in front of him.

No, thought Jenny, you are the feminine one.

*

The Villa

Civility is the cement of a relationship. Once Jenny jeered at Ahmed's pottery, 'The primitive style wouldn't you say? Primitive!' Once he told her that her thighs wobbled. They spent much of their days trying to escape each other. As Jenny watched Ahmed approaching the house she would flee through the side door. Waiting for Richard to come home from the office had been one of the great pleasures of her marriage. Even when she was unsure of his mood, his return had had a heroic quality. There had been two natural points to her day: Richard leaving in the morning and Richard returning in the evening. Now she and Ahmed wound their way round each other like cats, never free of each other.

One day Jenny found her few bits of good jewellery, mostly inherited from Richard's mother, had gone from her bedside drawer along with the three euros that Jessica had handed her the night before.

Jenny went to find Jessica who was working on some tapestry on the oddly shaped patio at the back of the house.

'My jewellery has gone,' she said flatly.

Jessica looked up and bit off a piece of thread.

'Ahmed's gone also,' she said with mild curiosity.

'Oh God,' said Jenny.

Jessica tipped back her head and shut her eyes.

'This is life. Ahmed has gone back to his own girl. He wasn't correct for you, Jenny. I thought he might have been, but finally I could not trust him. He would not do what he was asked. And evidently he is a thief as well.'

'Shall I call the police?' asked Jenny dully.

'I don't think so, no. For what purpose? He is gone. Maybe he is a thief, perhaps he is a murderer for all that we know. It is better that he is gone. *Alors*, Jenny, the two of us are alone now. I want this to last, I think we will be happy together for a while.'

Jenny felt the fight go out of her. Very well, they would be two village spinsters. The drawbridge to her old life had gone up. She was not afraid of what would become of her here, not afraid of loneliness or even death. What she could not bear was the thought of Emily, who had stood innocently and composedly listening to her mother reject her. Jenny's love for Emily had always seemed too big for her, now the slightest memory of it was a furnace. Emily appeared in Jenny's dreams as an other worldy figure, an avenging angel.

Much better the dull misery of life with Jessica, a routine of breakfast and housework and watching quizzes on an old black and white television and lying together at night. Jenny gave small groans and sighs under Jessica's rough embraces until she awoke and realized it was not Richard. Then she pulled down her nightdress and turned on her side.

The Villa

She was good at cooking and cleaning. She took in ironing and mending from the village. She would make an accomplished wife for Richard, had he read her enhanced CV in her letters. Jenny found the tone of her correspondence difficult to get right. She had tried abject – 'God knows what you must think of me'; cute – 'I cannot manage on my own, I need you to tell me what to do'; dramatic – 'If I live that long . . .'; curt – 'Is it easier if I talk direct to the solicitor?; and after a while, awkward. Jenny always thought the greatest achievement of marriage was intimacy. 'I know you *so* well,' she used to say to Richard, who sometimes gave a slight shudder. It was strange how you could unknow somebody. The shared experience, humour, child, had left no residual connection at all. She felt she had more in common with the village butcher than with Richard. Perhaps if she heard his voice she would have felt him more. If she heard Emily's voice her heart would slice in two. But Richard was ex-directory now and Jenny's only communication was on pale blue writing paper, stamped with Jessica's address, and set out most correctly, in the secretarial fashion – Dear Richard, Yours sincerely.

Once she wrote Dear Richard, only to cross it out and start Dear Toby. She hesitated and said the name out loud. Then her grip on her pen relaxed and she wrote quickly and fluently, page after page. She hoped this time she had got the tone right. No pressure. Easy come, easy go.

Dear Toby,

Well, long time no see, as the temps at work used to say. I am quite a native here now and am altogether au fait with French cooking. The key is to cook it slowly. In fact, I do everything slowly – I live slowly. In Chiswick I always thought about the big picture, but here I am a miniaturist. If I have completed a piece of sewing or made a really good chicken in the pot, I am quite satisfied.

But much more interesting, how are you??? And how are you getting on at Edinburgh? I do hope that is where you have ended up. If you went to Durham or Dublin, this letter won't reach you for a start! But I have a kind of telepathic feeling about you, Toby. You are the only solid ground. If you don't get this letter then . . .

Anyhow, let's not go into all that! I would just like to hear how things are. What is the student accommodation like? I wonder if it is a bit of a shock going from a comfortable room with a proper mattress and en suite facilities to a pretty basic room with cheap furniture and a bathroom down the corridor. But we learn to live in different conditions. We all adapt, don't we, in our fashion. I mean you can't expect the good life for ever.

I suppose it depends on your definition of a good

life. That is how some people might describe France. You might think more sunshine and no cars and fresh food is a recipe for a good life. Although funnily enough it is much healthier in Chiswick because one does proper exercise in a gym, which tones all your muscles. Walking and heaving things about doesn't do the right things in the right places I find. Oh, and the sunshine creases your skin. And come to think of it, the cold is much worse. And the food may be better, but how boring to eat those slow stews without company. Just me and Jessica, our jaws sawing and juicing.

ANYWAY! I don't want you to think I am down. It is so important to make the best of things, don't you think? Isn't that what I always used to say to you? I remember watching you play football for your school and you were on the subs bench and I said to you, 'Don't sulk, just show them what you can do with what you have been given!' Do you remember? Only unfortunately you never got onto the pitch during that game. It broke my heart watching you smiling and doing your exercises in anticipation. Brave face, eh Toby? Always a brave face.

Anyhow! I hope Richard and Emily are OK. They are much too busy to reply to my letters!!! I think Richard is a bit off me, and as for Emily, well, you know what girls are like! One minute you are their best friend, then they don't want to know. It was the same with the girls in the office. I haven't heard from them in years. Do you know if Emily is still playing the piano?

Hey! I mustn't ramble on. It is so good to be in touch with you. I would love to hear all your news and just to know Emily is OK and not being bullied or, you know, taking drugs or anything. That she is safe. That is what I pray for each night. God bless Emily and keep her safe, God bless Richard and keep him safe. God bless Toby and help him keep ME safe. Prodigal stepmother, eh Toby?

Still! I mustn't keep you. You have your own life to lead. I am so grateful to be part of your life, Toby. That is why I am writing to you. My Toby. My friend and my son.

Look after yourself! Don't worry about replying if you are very busy. I enclose a stamped addressed envelope. Here's hoping to hear from you a.s.a.p.

With love

Jenny

PS. Been on any good holidays?

Jenny took her bicycle which was balanced against the wall down to the post office. She had stopped using the car since it began making a scraping noise along the road. She had tried to ignore it but became self-conscious and feared the car would just pack up. Jenny had entertained the idea of driving the car at high speed off the road. She guessed correctly that it might make her family and friends more kindly disposed to her. But now she could not get the car to go at more than fifteen kilometres an hour. Nor could she afford to have it repaired. So she left it to rust outside the house and used Jessica's spare bicycle. She looked like a mad spinster all right. One of the tenants at the villa had said she reminded them of Muriel Spark. She may have meant well, but no woman who valued her hairdresser would take that as a compliment.

Jenny's certainty in Toby started to fade after a fortnight and she watched the postman speed up the frosty track with hopeless equanimity. Then one dry, windy morning three weeks later as she was sweeping up the leaves, Jessica tapped her on the shoulder.

'From Edinburgh, that must be Toby, I think,' she said. Jenny avoided looking at Jessica's face, at her knowing amber-coloured eyes, at the gullies down her cheeks caused by relentless smoking. It occurred to Jenny that while she was responsible for her actions, she had ended up a prisoner.

'Thank you, I'll open it later,' she said, placing it on the round stone table by the door.

'But for sure, you want to look now,' said Jessica reaching for the letter.

'No! No thank you, it can wait until I finish this,' cried Jenny flailing at the ground with her birch broom.

'*Alors*,' cried Jessica, clutching a supporting pillar as a whining tunnel of wind almost toppled her; Jenny raised her arms like a scarecrow and shut her eyes against the sudden squall. When she opened them, she saw the white envelope waltzing over the roof of the house.

'Get it! Oh get it! My letter,' she shrieked as it soared as if by suction further and further away over the trees.

Both women watched, like wooden figures.

Then Jenny ran inside and threw herself onto the bedspread, her hoarse sobbing muffled by the damask.

She felt a hand and then lips on the back of her neck.

'It does not matter. Toby says what you want him to say. His letter will be like a mirror. What you ask him, he answers, my dear.'

Jenny slowly rolled herself on to her back, wiping her nose with her sleeve producing a gluey smear over her cheek.

She stretched out her arms.

'I think he was asking me to visit him. Will you give me a break? I will return. Of course I will Jess darling.'

Twelve

Edinburgh

It was midday when Toby emerged from his room in track-suit bottoms and a baggy, once white T-shirt, his thick, dark hair standing on end, and shuffled into the bathroom. He took a tube of toothpaste and a brush from the chipped cupboard and scrubbed his teeth expressionlessly in front of the oval, pock-marked mirror. The garish blue of the walls gave an unflattering light to the room and an unhealthy tint to Toby's complexion. He looked both dingy and profoundly handsome.

'Tobes! Tobes, mate – phone,' came a rusty voice from the bottom of the stairs.

Toby slid one hand into his baggy pocket and felt his cell phone. He spat a pool of foamy white into the basin and called back.

'What phone? For me?'

'It's the payphone. Some woman. Stop being such a lazy

bastard and come down here. What are you doing up there –
wanking?'

Toby jogged along the corridor, arms bent as if on an
athletic track, and stepped lightly down the stairs. He picked
up the old-fashioned black phone swinging on its cord in the
booth at the back of the hallway. On the shelf were a stack of
torn and incomplete motorcycle and pornographic magazines.
Above it someone had doodled on the wall: 'If you are dreaming you are living, think about it.' Beneath it was the reply:
'I can't, I'm asleep.'

'Hey?' said Toby.

'Toby? It's me. Long time, no see.'

Toby lifted his arm in a loose bowling gesture, while
cupping the phone against his other shoulder.

'Aunt Sal?'

'Jenny! It's Jenny! You said to drop by didn't you? Well, I
have! I'm at the train station. What shall I do now?'

Toby became unusually still, the muscles in his back
clenching so that a central panel of his T-shirt became trapped
into a crease.

'Did I say drop by? I thought I just said have a nice life.'

'Can't hear, there's a train announcement. What shall I do?'

'If you're here, can you get a taxi?'

'Of course. If that's what you want me to do. You'll be
there to meet me? Which building are you in?'

Toby gave the address while shaking his head slightly and

looking down at the little black tuft of hair on his foot. It reminded him of his old hamster.

He had definitely written 'maybe in a few years and hey, have a nice life'. This was maybe in a few weeks. He sighed. Poor dumb woman, she had messed up everything, you had to feel sorry for her. Someone had to look after her and it might as well be him.

He replaced the receiver and blinked at it, before walking slowly back up the stairs. Midway he began to take two at a time.

As he opened the bedroom door a sci-fi rope of light shone from wall to wall illuminating somersaulting particles of dust. A curly head turned on the pillow.

Toby crouched down and ran his hand tenderly over it.

'Hey, Daisy?' he whispered. 'I guess you should wake up. Jenny is coming over.'

When Jenny was having her affair with Richard, she would make a point of choosing cute presents for Toby to accentuate her lovability rather than Toby's. One needs a practical everyday relationship with a child in order to be precise about size and interests. The crew-necked, cable-stitched cashmere sweater with the French label was a squeeze, but then the smaller Toby was, the more confident Jenny had felt. Then there were the naughty presents, flick knives or pellet guns, which Jenny handed over with a swaggering apology. The Martha Gellhorn style presents were naturally designed to emphasize the timidity of Richard's home life.

At Edinburgh station, Jenny bought a greasy-looking teddy bear with a tartan necktie. Her instincts for emotional bribery were too deep to rationalize.

There he was, that was him, standing outside the railings of a handsome grey town house as if he was the last child to be picked up from school, hands in pockets, a woollen hat pushed down over his dark head, muscular arms folded. How had he grown up like that? 'You will understand better when you're older,' Richard had said and Jenny had smiled sadly across the hotel table at the slight boy in school uniform all those years ago. Jenny's mind was like a hyperactive video machine whizzing backwards and forwards.

She was surprised by the bare scruffiness of the house inside. For an out of focus second she had imagined Toby had whizzed through another twelve years and was welcoming her into his gracious family home. Instead she met a cluster of slouching, anaemic-looking girls with their trousers sagging below their knickers. Jenny had never seen student life before. She had gone straight from school to office and understood punctuality and tidiness. She had always experienced partitioned days. Yet here she was, standing in wilful poverty, surrounded by pale creatures making meals in mugs and wandering in and out of each other's bedroom, as if sex had no consequences. It was an offensive opt out from real life. At least her own life was not suspended, just ruined.

Jenny's flash of moral indignation made her neck glow. Just as shoplifters feel entitled to what others buy, so Jenny was overcome with the moral impulse to condemn somebody else. Why shouldn't she?

As she inhaled and turned her back on the Cup-a-Soup brigade, one of them, plumper and more outward than the rest, called out from the gloom, 'Hello, Jenny, you have come a long way.'

Jenny peered back. Her eyesight had deteriorated in the last couple of years, too much scanning of the horizon and too many lamps.

'Daisy?' she faltered.

Toby went over and squeezed Daisy to him, so that his biceps grew rounder and flatter. Jenny gave a flatulent sigh.

'Just dropping by.' She grinned.

'So, who else were you seeing in Edinburgh?' asked Daisy.

Jenny tried to answer, but her lips could not begin to form words. They felt anaesthetized. She thought that if she said anything it might well tumble out in the wrong order as if she were a stroke victim. She felt that all her strength and sanity had been used up just getting here. It was for Toby to decide what happened to her now.

'Er, what about a cup of coffee?' asked Daisy, exchanging a look with Toby which said, This woman is seriously weird.

Why had Jenny spent ten caressing married years on the verge of tears and now that she had become pitiful, her eyes were as dry as dust? She smiled like a mime artist at Daisy.

'I'm just catching up with friends. Hearing how the festival went this year. And I thought I would check up on you two. Might need to report back to your mother, you never know.' She leered at Daisy.

'Do you know my mum?' asked Daisy puzzled. 'Oh, I guess Richard must have filled you in about everything.'

Jenny could feel Toby's eyes on her. He was keeping his distance. He hadn't kissed her, couldn't even touch her hand. She thought of his childish thrashing form in bed with her on her honeymoon. He was the one person who had always given Jenny the benefit of the doubt, the one who had really seemed to like her. What was his expression now? Kindly embarrassment? Pity? Contempt? All those things wrapped in an emotional weariness. He had had enough of her dramas. Toby wished she wasn't here, wished she could be somebody else's problem. From now on, thought Jenny, as panicky as a bird caught down a chimney, I am a burden on those I love. Love is conditional after all. It expects high and consistent standards of behaviour. It will not tolerate ugly, selfish behaviour, however out of character. Presentation matters.

'Yes, yes, I like to keep in touch with what's going on.

And now, I do hope you won't think me rude, but this was only a flying visit. I have so much to pack in. Come and see us in France, it'll be good for you both. Such fun! I am counting on Emily coming out for Christmas! Make sure you eat the right things!' said Jenny (or you could try doing without anything to eat, she thought, with a last critical glance at Daisy).

'But you've only just arrived!' said Daisy, both surprised and relieved.

'I can't miss the next train. Don't see me out, honestly. Love you and leave you!'

'Who is us?' said Toby.

'What?' said Jenny, buttoning up her coat and stalking towards the door.

'You said, "Come and see us in France."'

'Goodbye, dearie,' whispered Jenny. She threw herself at a passing taxi and rocked back onto the seat. The teddy bear fell out of her straw bag and onto the floor.

'To the station,' she said. She glimpsed her waxy face in the driver's rear mirror and smiled politely back at it.

There was a feature of celebrity magazine interviews on which Jenny had always fastened: the actresses would protest that age held no terrors for them. They felt more womanly, sexier, freer than ever before. Yes, until you go and stand next to a twenty-year-old, Jenny thought, rolling her eyes. In which case you look tired, old, fussy, embarrassing. And the thing was that the young, for all their self-consciousness, had no sense of the effect they had on others. Maybe indulgence and admiration were like air to them. How could Daisy know that her careless physical optimism had a shrivelling effect on Jenny, that it had made her own hopes for the future preposterous.

What Jenny had planned to discuss with Toby was her move back to England. Her bag was heavy with brochures for cottages to rent, both holiday lets and longer-term contracts. She had registered an interest with every major English estate agent. Some had got wise and threatened to remove her from their books. Then she had written to them in a trembling hand: 'My circumstances are about to change and my search for an English property has become urgent.'

Brochures from England, and the BBC's world service, had kept Jenny sane. She loved to hear about those non-holiday-type places. She felt a sympathy with their unlovability. Moreover, any place name pronounced with an English accent choked her. Of course she was sad and lonely, but most of all she was homesick. Her holiday had become an exile. It was as if her plane had been delayed for a year. She realized, as she wandered round Edinburgh station trying to make sense of the announcement boards, that place was not the point. People were.

Defeated, she leant her temple against the cold train window, her scarf pulled up over her face, her eyes closed in order to avoid her reflection. When she had first started seeing Richard he had laughingly upbraided her for automatically checking her appearance in shop windows.

'There, you've done it again!' he would accuse her, their arms swinging, their hands joined.

'I wasn't. I was looking at the shop front ... yes, I was.' She would laugh back sheepishly. Then she married him and concentrated on keeping up appearances. Then she left him and avoided appearances. She squeezed her eyes tighter when the train entered the tunnel in a rush of wind.

So this was Plan B – a visit to Richard's solicitor in Edgware. He had once seemed kind, or at least impartial towards her. Her expectations of other people had grown so modest that anything warmer than shuddering revulsion made her grateful. Only in Toby had she felt limitless hope.

The solicitor was courteous, explaining patiently that she was not entitled to more than a lump sum of £15,000. He produced her signature at the end of five pages of clauses. Jenny had stumbled down the steep steps from his office.

'Are you OK there?' the secretary had called after her. Presumably it was part of her job to prevent foolish ex-wives from throwing themselves down stairs.

Jenny thought about going to Emily's school, but her head felt inflamed at the prospect of ranks of disapproval. She had developed a distaste for drama. She spent the night in a grimy hotel in Earl's Court, among asylum seekers. She liked her brown carpet, small sink and grubby windowsill. It was her room. No one could find her, nobody cared for her. She could disappear here. But something, either habit or self-respect, she did not know which, propelled her to rise the next day and get dressed in unclean clothes, pay her bill and walk to the tube station.

Jenny was shaking with tiredness by the time she arrived back at Jessica's villa. Failure is a kind of homecoming.

That winter, Jenny felt her old self had been finally extinguished. The moment of defeat does not always follow struggle. Sometimes it is effortless realization.

It was merely that her daily routine – cycling to the shops, cleaning, sewing and, as the light faded, keeping Jessica company – became her substantial existence. Her family were a memory now, a war wound she no longer fussed over. Jessica did not like her to mention them. She had once found Jenny doubled up on the floor gasping at a pain she could not locate.

'It must be the moon,' Jessica had said drily. 'You have disappeared in the head. No wonder Richard wanted to fuck the accountant. But it is no matter, I will be tender to you.' Frightened, grateful and enraged, Jenny said nothing. If an image of Emily or Toby or Richard subsequently escaped into her head she stood still and breathed deeply, her eyes closed until she had repulsed it, like nausea. She was no longer separated from Emily, she was bereaved. She spoke of her in the past tense. Her old yoga teacher had come in useful. Mind over matter. Mind over love.

After two more years, she one day returned from the shops with Jessica and realized this was not a misadventure but her future. She had overheard the latest family at the villa describe her and Jessica as a couple of crazy old dykes, and this did not seem inaccurate. British visitors treated her with a polite awkwardness, but she got on fine with their children. The ones she liked best were girls of about eight or nine. When she popped by to check that the water was working and there had been no breakages she would carry some coins to throw in the pool for the children to dive for.

'You must let Jenny go,' mothers called out to their daughters, and Jenny would wink fiercely. She was in no hurry. The girls who were affectionate were allowed to accompany her to the shed at the edge of the wood where she made her pottery. She would let the most sensible and the sweetest make imprints of their hands, which they painted in bright colours. The surfaces were covered with abandoned, childish shapes. Once, a mother had followed them and peered through the small vine-covered window. Jenny had risen with dignity and opened the door, blocking part of the entrance with her skinny form.

'This is very good of you,' the woman had said, glancing suspiciously round the side of her. 'Do you have daughters yourself?'

Jenny had shaken her head, and ushered the girl out of her work place. She had not been invited again. Her protégées were not only sensible and sweet, they had to keep secrets.

One day, after Jenny had seen a family off – their luggage blocking the back seat of the car, hands, of which there were moulds, waving – she had folded her arms, shivered despite the heat, and shut herself in the shed. Beneath a sheet was her special project, a life-sized clay girl, her knees bent, her hands together and her arms stretched above her head. Jenny traced the bump of a swimming costume with her dirty, broken fingernail. Her face was serene. France had cured her of her nervous grimaces. Her nerves were disconnected from her heart.

Outside there was the noise of wheels on gravel. Jenny frowned and threw the sheet back over her diver. They always forgot something. It was one of Jenny's duties to wrap up discarded swimming costumes, damp and dusty, or beloved, abandoned soft toys and take them to the post office with an accompanying note sprinkled with exclamation marks. She walked back up to the terrace, her smile ready. A tall well-featured young man appeared, watching her.

Jenny wiped a hand across her face

'Toby?' she said.

'Thought I'd pay a return visit,' he said, settling himself

down at the table with the ease of the innocent. He threw down his mobile phone and wallet and took off his denim jacket.

'It hasn't changed here,' he said.

'That's the thing about holiday homes, they are set in aspic,' Jenny cried gaily as she fussed over him with cups and saucers and plates of almond cakes.

'You've changed, though,' said Toby pleasantly. Jenny bowed her head. In two years she had become aged and plain, that was the Mediterranean way. There was no need for him to explain.

'And look at you – so handsome,' she said, pinching his arm. He gave a reserved smile. He had been reserved when he could have been fond and now he was reserved when he could have been hostile. It was an admirably transferable quality.

'And how is the family?' she asked, grateful that her parched eyes could no longer produce tears.

'Good,' said Toby, his white teeth sinking into a cake. 'Dad's remarried.'

'Yes, yes, good,' said Jenny, wiping crumbs from the table with a trembling hand. 'Anyone I know?'

'Daisy's mum actually,' said Toby, turning his face to the sun.

'Ah. Not Amanda then.'

'Amanda? No, she's married to Derek,' said Toby with a puritanical straightforwardness. 'Actually, we see quite a bit of them.'

259

'We?'

'Daisy and me. We're still together. Might even get hitched. What do you think?'

'Ah. What a merry-go-round.'

'I wanted to say thanks, actually. Hope that doesn't sound too egocentric. We keep saying to each other, if it hadn't been for that holiday . . .'

'You can't be serious about getting married,' said Jenny in a cracked voice.

Toby leaned forward, his elbow on his knee. Jenny took in every contour of his face and body so she would remember it later.

When she spoke to him it was as if from a dream. 'I mean, after everything you learnt from us?'

'Learnt? From you guys? Well, I learnt that I want to get married to a girl I love and that I will be faithful to her. I mean that. And I want to have kids and stuff, somewhere down the line. Did you think you could put me off? Come on, Jenny, it's the only thing. I've seen how precious it all is. Emily is my best mate. The fact that you couldn't hack it, doesn't mean I can't give it a shot. I was there, I saw what you threw away. It was fucking paradise.'

'Toby! Don't swear!'

Toby leant back in his chair. Jenny stared at his wide, sculpted chest. Here was a beautiful man who wanted to behave well. Not bang women against walls with their legs hitched like dogs. Not sweaty or drunk or sly. Not looking for action in the office. He wanted to honour one woman. Well, good luck to him. God bless him. Let's hope Daisy had the same ideals. Let her never feel bored or distracted or pissed or promiscuously lustful. Let it be a marriage without holidays.

'What about you? You OK? Ahmed?' asked Toby politely, as if showing interest in someone's bizarre hobby.

'Ooh no, no, that didn't last,' said Jenny pouring some more tea. 'I live with Jessica now. I help out here. I'm fine really, it's rather interesting.'

Toby lifted his sunglasses and yawned. He reached for his phone.

'Well, I just thought I'd call by. Daisy and I are staying in Marseille. We're going on to Spain.'

'Toby?'

'Yep,' he said, putting on his jacket.

'You mentioned Emily.'

He looked at Jenny. 'She's cool. She's well.'

'Do you have . . .?'

'Yeah, I brought some pictures from her birthday. They had a disco sleepover, dressed up.'

Jenny took the packet of photographs, her fingers arthritic with tension.

'Can I keep them?'

'Sure. You want to look at them now? You might not know which one . . .'

Jenny gave a grunt of pain.

'I'll look at them a bit later.'

She put the shiny yellow folder into her front pocket.

'Will you call again Toby? With Daisy?'

'We're moving on tomorrow.'

'Yes, of course. Send my love to her.'

Toby bent down to kiss Jenny on the cheek. She held herself stiffly until he had gone. Then she sat down and opened the folder.

Toby was right. The girls, who were heavily made-up, had the uniformity of a chorus line. But there was something tearingly familiar about the folded arms of the girl on the left: skinny, defiant arms. Her hair was longer, but the snub nose and square jaw were Emily's. Jenny traced the face with her finger. As the light faded and the noises of frogs and birds and the wind grew louder, a harsher sound of a wailing mother carried over the valley.

It was dark when Jenny returned to the small house on the hill. Jessica was sitting inside at the table filling in forms for the next family to arrive.

'Is that you, Jenny?' she said. 'Where have you been? Leaving me with everything. You are not pushing your weight, Jenny. There is plenty to do here. You could make us some coffee for a start.'

The Villa

Jenny appeared in the doorway, coat on, carrying a large clay sculpture.

'What in heaven is that? What are you doing with that?'

'Just something I made for the garden,' said Jenny quietly.

'What is it? A dog? Oh, I see, no, it is a swimmer. It is your daughter, no? It is Emily.'

Jenny placed the clay statue down on the floor.

'Will it be in your way, Jessica? I'll put it in the garden in the morning.'

'OK, put it in the garden. It looks like a gravestone anyway, my dear.'

'What did you say?'

'Whose gravestone, I wonder? Now I have been sharpening the knives all day. What shall we cook for our dinner? Something special, to celebrate our life together, no?'

Jenny walked over to the window and looked at the darkening sky. She clasped her hands together.

'God bless Emily, God bless Toby, God bless Richard, and Mum and Dad. And our Father, which art in heaven, hallowed be thy name, thy Kingdom come, thy will be done, on earth as it is in heaven. And give us this day our daily bread, and forgive us our trespasses . . .'

Jessica was close behind her.

'Shh, that is enough now,' she whispered. 'It is enough now.'